3448

WHAT ABOUT TOMORROW

Ivan Southall

WHAT ABOUT TOMORROW

Macmillan Publishing Co., Inc.

New York

Macmillan Publishing Co., Inc.
866 Third Avenue, New York, N.Y. 10022
Collier Macmillan Canada, Ltd.
First American edition, 1977
Printed in the United States of America
10 9 8 7 6 5 4 3 2 1

LIBRARY OF CONGRESS CATALOGING IN PUBLICATION DATA

Southall, Ivan.   What about tomorrow.

SUMMARY: In Australia during the Depression, a fourteen-year-old boy runs away from home after a bike accident and sets in motion events that will determine his future.

[1. Australia—Fiction. 2. Runaways—Fiction. 3. Depressions—1929—Fiction] I. Title.
PZ7.S726Wh3   [Fic]   76-45637   ISBN 0-02-786170-8

To Elizabeth

Books by Ivan Southall

MACMILLAN PUBLISHING CO., INC.

Josh
Head in the Clouds
Benson Boy
Matt and Jo
Hills End
Seventeen Seconds
Fly West
A Journey of Discovery
What About Tomorrow

ST. MARTIN'S PRESS, INC.

Ash Road
The Curse of Cain
Let the Balloon Go
Sly Old Wardrobe (with Ted Greenwood)
Finn's Folly
Chinaman's Reef Is Ours

BRADBURY PRESS, INC.

Walk a Mile and Get Nowhere

WHAT ABOUT TOMORROW

One

If ever Sam's adventure began—in the sense of beginning—it was on the day that he hit the tram: August 11, 1931.

It was about 4:30 and raining a fine mist; drops trickling from Sam's hair and drops on his eyelashes and drops running down his neck—funny how memories of the kind can stick. Everything was gray and cold, as if the street lights should have been turned on to warm things up, but Sam was whistling some tune or other, a terrible-sounding thing he was putting together as he went along. You know—breathing in and breathing out! Tone deaf, he was; utterly tone deaf. Music coming out of Sam was a disaster, but he was a cheerful kid generally, or else a small screw loose. Any kid zipping down Riversdale Road on a bicycle on an afternoon like that, whistling his head off as if the world were a great place, had to be addled in the brain, at least a bit. And Sam was that. Oh yes, he was that.

Heaven knows what he thought of the world, though. Probably as a misty place full of alien creatures and other strange objects that little by little he had been catching glimpses of through the fog—that fog out of which all young and growing things must emerge before others can see them, or they can see anything very clearly for themselves. Well, that's the way Sam's learned friends would have put it, I'm pretty sure (and he did pick up a few learned friends along the route). Sam himself would have been more likely to say, "What do I think of the world? Gawd. What you asking me that kind of question for? You think I'm Einstein or Newton or something?"

From the day he was born, according to Dad, the things that made up Sam's life had been vague. And from a man's point of view that was a pretty good definition. Vague. But Dad had reached the vague stage himself by then.

Things happened, of course, all around Sam. Did they ever! Buildings fell down, bridges collapsed, lightning struck, gas mains blew up, but never when Sam was there in person. He'd either just gone home, hadn't arrived yet, or had changed his mind and gone somewhere else. That was how it was with Sam, for most of his life, except when it came to the crunch.

Everyone at home used to say that if you wanted Sam to remember anything, you told him twice; if you wanted to attract his attention, you shouted twice; if you wanted him to do anything, such as get up in the morning or comb his hair or even go to bed at night, you kept on yelling and hoped for the best. Strange how wearing it could be; strange how it used to wear people out; strange how they actually enjoyed the peace when he didn't come home for a bit. Yeh; they missed him; of course they missed him; but not all that much!

Sam never noticed things, I guess, or else never rested long enough from rushing here and there to open his eyes and take a proper look. Well, not before August 11, 1931. I can't say that Dad expected more; perhaps his expectations were not high enough, but that was his way. He'd been knocked around too much himself. He was not looking for anyone in the family (not even the aunts and uncles and cousins) to lead the revolution. There was nothing wrong, he used to say, with a growing boy spending half his life in a trance, and a hell of a lot to commend it. Why go begging for the world to knock your block off while there was still a chance of ducking and letting the blow pass by over the top? But you don't hear Dad saying it any more: the dead don't talk.

Sleep well, Dad. Sleep tight. Or else wake up over there and find things right.

Sam—fourteen years, four months, and eight days. A nicely rounded age, wouldn't you say, for hitting a tram?

Sam—in the ninth grade, five feet eight inches tall (likely to go five inches taller if he managed to stay alive until he grew up—not a certainty, some used to reckon), light-boned, light in every way actually, but winner of one ferocious fistfight behind the incinerator at school. And I mean ferocious, mate; oh my gosh, do I ever. Sam got a lot of respect after that; they hadn't guessed he had it in him. Never kissed a girl though, even if a couple of encounters had narrowly failed. The girl got the panics and ran away, making Sam twice as scared as she was herself. Same girl each time. Her name was Rose.

Sam—second child of two, living at 14 Wickham Street when he was at home, sleeping out on the back veranda where the rain blew in and the canvas blind slapped with ragged ends and the mosquitoes had a picnic. After a stifling hot night when a fellow lay there uncovered, he used to wake in the morning all swollen and looking like a bad case of acne. And bet your life Auntie would say, "That boy's getting too many sweets."

Which was a stupid thing to say; he hardly ever got his hands on a sweet, and would rather have bought a hot potato cake anyway.

"That boy's getting too much pocket money."

Which was ridiculous. He got none at all, and handed over all his earnings, except the few pence he could fiddle for himself on his paper round—and that went on potato cakes at a ha'penny a time.

"That boy's got kidney trouble. All puffy round the eyes. You'd better have his water tested."

It was terribly embarrassing having to put up with her. Singing in the church choir on Sundays looking holy, looking like some lady missionary just home from Fiji, which wasn't that far from the truth, and the rest of the week sounding so crude.

"That boy looks most unhealthy."

Which was a shocking exaggeration, but Auntie always made the most of everything. That was the story of her life, poor dear. As Dad said, what else had life to offer her except a bit of exaggeration?

There was Sam, zipping down Riversdale Road hill with sixty-four evening *Herald*s bulging in burlap bags over the bar of his bicycle and the tram stopped. Not that he noticed it straightaway—or, maybe, for a vital instant, he forgot!

It was not too difficult riding a bike without brakes as long as you remembered you were riding a bike without brakes—one of those smart aphorisms that had a lot of truth in it. You came into corners slower and downhill dragged your feet or got over into the gravel edges (if there were any) and broadsided your speed off. Sometimes you shot up side streets, or if things turned desperate, rocketed off the road onto the verge, hurdling the gutter like a steeplechaser. You could bail out then, you could jump for it, and land on your chest or kneecaps or the back of your head. Passers-by used to gape or shriek or rush to pick Sam up. It was amazing how hard he could come down without breaking himself in little pieces or completely wrecking the bike.

Dad had had the bike when he was a kid. Old Man Vale at the bike shop said it couldn't be fixed any more. He had been fixing it off and on at a shilling a time for thirty years. You'd reckon, you know, you really would, that having fixed it for so long he'd have accepted that he was stuck with it, and that there was no dodging it, and that it had to be done. But what did he do? "It doesn't need a new hub," he said, "or a new anythin'. I keep tellin' your dad, young Sam, it's no good sendin' you in here any more. It's worn out, boy. The whole thing's shot. Your grandfather bought it off me in 1899 and that's not yesterday—as I know better than most. Everythin' needs to be new sometime, and everythin' needs to be put away sometime."

"Gawd, Mr. Vale," Sam said, "are you askin' me to do without me bike?"

"I'm not asking you to do anything," that old man said, betraying his life's trust. "I'm tellin' you what I won't do. I'm not fixing it any more."

Sam's voice started turning thin and whiny. Do you blame him? "But what about me paper round, Mr. Vale? And what about getting to school? Two flipping miles. And I've got places to go, and things to do. I've got me life to live, Mr. Vale."

"Try putting your feet to the ground, Sam. Try walking for a change."

"Gawd, y'don't know what you're saying."

"Yes, I do, Sam. You put one foot down and swing the other leg past it and away you go. It's amazing. It's magic. It works. I've been doing it for seventy years. Don't you ride that bike no more, boy. No kid of mine would be riding it. No kid of mine, Sam."

The emptiness of the thought. The emptiness of standing there, poor Sam just standing there, just thinking about it. Like black night falling at eleven in the morning.

"Look, Mr. Vale. You just gotta fix it. Without me bike I'm nothing."

He could have sworn the tram was still moving, but that

tram was standing there, stationary, putting people down. People were getting off the thing and walking to the curb. So Sam jammed on the brake and the brake wasn't there.

Oh my gawd. That rotten old man.

"OUT OF ME WAY."

But no one took a blind bit of notice. There was Sam screaming his head off, ringing his bell, dragging a foot on the road, newspapers tossing him off balance, slipping and slithering on the shiny wet road, and nowhere in the world—or the time—to go anywhere except into the back of the tram.

There was a crunching sound, like a steamroller running over stones. The bike took off from under him as if someone had whipped it away. Away it went, flying away, bits falling off it, newspapers showering everywhere like elephant-sized confetti, Sam himself making a horrible sound.

That's what life does to you, mate. Suddenly lets you know it's time.

There was Sam underneath the tram wrapped about a wheel, underneath the guardrails, as if he had been ironed out flat and pushed through.

Two

PEOPLE WERE discussing a mishap. Sam was there somewhere.

"Is he dead?"

"How'd he get *in there*?"

"Looks like the *Herald* boy that does up by the station."

"Is he dead?"

"How d'you get him out, for cryin' out loud?"

"Silly little fool. Frightening the life out of everybody."

"Do you reckon he's alive?"

"Come on, kid. Get a wriggle on. Out you come."

"Can we lift the tram, do you reckon?"

"Look at the bike he was riding. Take a look at it, will you. Here, did you see this bike? Tied up with bits of wire. There ought to be a law against it."

"Give us a go at the running board. Come on, you people, we're not getting anywhere. Maybe we can wrench it off."

"You go easy on my tram, mate."

"What about jacking it up then? D'you carry tools for lifting it up?"

"What for? Why would I carry tools for lifting up a tram?"

"You've got a kid under there."

"I know I've got a kid under there. But I don't get kids under me tram every day, do I? Carry a jack for getting kids out? You're not serious, mate."

"Hey, you! You there, walking over his newspapers! Have a heart. The kid'll have to pay for them. Why don't you gather them up for him instead of plastering your dirty great hoofs all over them? Hey, kid. Can you hear me? Hey, kid, give us your hand, come on, and I'll pull you out."

"Lucky his back's not broken. Lucky he's not dead. Silly little fool. Riding like a lunatic."

They were peeling him away from the steel wheel like skins from an onion. That was what it felt like. As if they were peeling him away and layers of Sam were being left behind. Sam, Sam, the onion man.

"Easy does it there. Go easy on the kid. Don't go straightening him like that before you're sure."

"Yeh, yeh, slide him out the way he is. God knows what's broken inside him."

Oh, what a lovely thought for a nice wet evening. Did they have to shout it out loud? Couldn't they have whispered it behind their hands? Couldn't they have not said it at all?

Sliding him out they were, away from the steel wheel, out into the open, back into the rain.

At least there'd been a bit of shelter under there.

Out in the rain again. Getting rained on like a seed on the ground. Gawd, there was a lot of rain coming down.

Faces up on top, all around. Boots down here, all around. Like being aged two again, in a playpen with bars. Fancy thinking of that. I mean, fancy being able to *remember*. Aged two? Maybe three? But would you be in a playpen at three years of age?

The *bars*. Nothing else. Nothing else remembered. Just the bars and your face pressed through.

"Are you all right, kid?" Someone went on asking it, as if a fellow would know! They were doing the looking, weren't they? Couldn't they see for themselves?

Hands started going over him; knobbly work-roughened hands, passing over his legs and ankles and wrists and arms, Sam not taking any part, just submitting. It was a long time since anyone had handled him. Years since Mum had touched anything but his feet. They were big, rough, gentle hands, but maybe pieces of him were breaking off just the same, maybe they were putting pieces to one side in a little heap. What a thought, oh my gawd—a tidy little heap of pieces put on one side. It would be awful if they got them muddled up and couldn't remember where to put them back again. Then they were unbuttoning his clothing and running over his body; those huge hands were pressing round his rib cage as if his body were an easy handful, Sam looking fearfully down expecting to see great lumps of raw flesh exposed.

"Does anything hurt, kid? Does anything feel wrong? You know, as if anything had been mucked up inside? Can you sit up, do you reckon? Would you like someone to take you home?"

"Button him up, mate, before he catches cold."

"Do you feel all right, kid?"

"He'll catch cold. He's wet through."

"Is he hurt bad, do you think? He hasn't said a word, has he?"

Strong arms carried him off the road. It was a church hall, or something of the kind, with steps at the edge of the pavement. They sat him on the steps with his chin in his hands, his teeth chattering, and a trembling starting in his belly as if parts of him were flapping round in a wind that was blowing inside.

"You're all right, kid. You're a lucky boy. But go easy until the shock wears off a bit. Keep yourself warm."

People were returning to the tram, looking back at him, then going inside. The driver and conductor were stamping on the damaged running board, jumping up and down on it as if in a hurry to make up lost time or anxious to escape. Two small boys in wet shiny black raincoats were peering at him from three or four yards away as if they had not seen anything like him before and were afraid to venture closer in case he roared like a lion or hissed like a snake. A woman with a cabbage and a wet *Herald* in a shopping basket was shrugging and walking off, clattering her heels. Other people were disappearing as if three-course dinners were going free in the next street. The gentle man with the hard-worked hands stood for a moment, one foot on the tram. "Take care, kid," he said; a sad-looking man, but smiling. Sam didn't want him to go, but the man went up inside and the bell jangled and away went the tram.

One small boy said, "What did you hit the tram for?"

The other small boy said, "Because he's a silly fool. You heard Mum say."

The woman with the *Herald* and the cabbage in the shopping basket called, "Come along, come along. You're standing in the rain."

Drops started dribbling from Sam's hair again, down his neck, and his bellyache had turned into something like a huge, hard ball. Blood was starting from his leg now, from abrasions, blood forcing its way out like sweat and going streaky and thin in the rain. Sharpness in his hip, too, inside his clothes; he ran his fingers gingerly down inside and everything felt sore and there were smears of blood when he brought up his hand. He looked at the blood on his hand, and looked at it, and looked at it, and then forgot what he was doing.

His bike was off the road, off it by a yard, where someone had dropped it down.

No use looking at that either. No good counting up the damage. It was done for, for good and all. Hard to realize; hard to make the leap into an empty world where he didn't have a bike any more. That wasn't some kind of nightmare years away—it was *now*.

How could he do his paper round?

How could he get to school?

How could he go picking blackberries with Rose?

How could he get to Sandringham to swim with his cousins in summertime?

All of life, all of it, suddenly changed.

You're nothing now, Sam.

Beside the bike were a few wet newspapers heaped up in a little stack of pulp, and two burlap bags. Other newspapers were on the road, scattered like litter after a football match, blown wide on gusts of wind before they had become too wet to blow, newspapers run over by the tram, walked over by people who had gone, sniffed at by dogs with muddy paws looking for scraps of food, and driven over as he watched by a Whippet tourer with a gray hood, a Thornycroft lorry with solid rubber tires, and a Morris Cowley.

Sixty-four *Herald*s, give or take a few.

Never in his whole life before had he realized how many *Herald*s sixty-four were.

If he lost one or went short in his money, the boss at the newspaper shop docked his pay.

Lumping sixty-four *Herald*s on his bike was bad enough, he knew he had a load, but nothing like sixty-four *Herald*s spread all over the road.

Eight shillings' worth of *Herald*s he was responsible for. Eight shillings or a hundred pounds. Just the same, when you earned sevenpence a day.

What about tomorrow?

Sam started crying from hurt and pain and fear. There was nothing else he knew how to do.

Three

SAM WASN'T the crying kind. Not at all. Crying wasn't being manly, people said, and being manly was terribly important, people said. Mum said it. Dad said it. Auntie said it. Crybaby. Crybaby. The kids up the street said it. The teachers at school said it. The preachers at church said it. Manliness was next to cleanliness, and cleanliness was next to godliness, and one was as good as another, it seemed, depending upon who said it. Tears were for girls who were allowed to let go whenever they chose. Just any old time at all. They could flood you out of house and home and no one cared. Being a girl must have been all right sometimes—exactly when being a boy was all wrong. Stiffen the upper lip, boy, they said; grit your teeth and hold on. Be a man for God and King and Country, and die with honor, boy, before you utter a whimper. Then God will love you and the girls will love you and you'll get the Victoria Cross—posthumously. Well, that was what it amounted to when you added it up.

So where did the tears come from? Oh, the shame of it. Dammed up for a lifetime, all those tears, flooding over with things not really troubled about before. Things like the hopelessness that lay in pools in Mum's eyes. Gray pools in her eyes, so deep they were deeper than Mum herself, as if wading into them you might sink out of sight. Oh, he feared for those pools now.

Things like that matter, Sam. There comes a day, that's what they say.

Yeh, maybe someone keeps the score. Yourself, perhaps, keeping it deep down where it doesn't get in the way, until suddenly up it comes flooding over the wall and you've got to face up to it fair and square. Everything you've ever avoided is still there, Sam. It never goes away. I mean, what a time to realize it; when your world's falling to bits.

"Would you like someone to take you home?" the man had said, then had gone off on the tram, as if he hadn't really meant it. Was he just making words, or did he have a job to get to on time, and couldn't be late for it, and couldn't risk his job for a kid, for any kid, not even for Sam sitting in the rain at the side of the road? Did he work at night, all night long, all alone, huddled at a factory gate shivering from cold, three o'clock in the morning shivering from cold, keeping watch to scare thieves away, dying, just dying, for daylight to come around so he could go home?

Yeh, he'd have a job to go to or he'd not be riding on a tram. People without jobs to go to put one foot down and swung the other leg past it like the old man said. Mum walked three miles to Camberwell to do her shopping, because things were cheaper there, then walked three miles home.

Sam would like someone to take him home, but no one came. Riversdale Road it was, not even nighttime, and no one stopped to say, "Hullo, kid; tell me about it." It must have been the rain, all that rain falling. People who would have been walking the streets stayed home or went round a more sheltered way.

It was hard remembering where home was. Definite things had gone vague and everything looked different without a bike to ride. Wickham Street was a thousand miles. Strange there being no people around, like a dream; no people, just rain, just shadows of people under shop verandas far away, as if they might have been there or not there and weren't even sure themselves and kept drifting between visible and invisible worlds.

In winter it was always rain, rain, rain. Was it the same about people? People not being around, except in the distance, except far away, unrealistically. Did kids who didn't have papers to deliver stay inside all warm looking out through net curtains and dribbles wandering on windowpanes? Not that way for Sam. Sam for three years riding his bike up and down blustery winter streets yelling *Herald* and pushing carefully rolled-up newspapers into letterboxes or sheltered pieces of pipe while his nose got colder and runnier and everything got wetter and his fingers turned so numb he could hardly count the change. Mistakes happening then and ending up short in his money that he had to pay back out of his earnings (after three whole years of working for that miserable man), meaning he could have been out in the wet for hours for fourpence maybe. For less than the price of three lousy papers! And Mum would say, "Oh, Sam. . . ." But nothing ever as bad as sixty-four *Herald*s to pay for. Nothing ever like this before. "Oh, Sam." He could hear her now. "I haven't got it, love. You work to bring money home, not to take it away. There's nowhere I can get eight shillings from; no way at all to pay that man."

"Look, Mr. Lynch," Sam would have to say. "I've lost your papers, eight shillings' worth, all over the road. And I've lost m'bike and I haven't got m'bike any more. And I've got gravel rash up and down me side. See for yourself, look at me, bleedin' an' all. Bits of me smeared all over the road."

Lynch peering down over his beak, rimless glasses perched there like a freaky-looking bird. "Eight shillings would buy a lot of petrol for my Chevrolet motorcar. Do you realize it'd take my family to the talkies and give us money over to buy ice creams?" (Well, he could say that. Why not? Every Thursday night off they went to the pictures, the whole bally lot of them, like they were the Royal Family or something.) "You'll have to work it off, kid." That's what he'd say. "What's it that you earn? Three shillings and sixpence a week. That's two weeks and two days you go on working before you get paid again, but how you're to manage that round without a bike, I'd like to know."

"Feet were made before bikes, Mr. Lynch. That's what they say. You put one foot down and swing the other one past it. You'll see."

"Don't know that I do see, boy. Kids have tried that round on foot long before you. Never saw them back till all hours. It's a bike round—that's what got you the job—*because* you had the bike. People can't go hanging round half the night for their papers to arrive. . . ."

What about Mum's stove waiting at home, waiting there this very minute, all that lovely heat waiting to happen, firebox door lying open for the sticks she'd push inside it. Fresh sticks blazing up, lovely roaring sounds in the flue, raindrops falling from the chimney to the hot plate and exploding into globules of splash and sizzle, everything smelling of steam and woodsmoke and drying clothes, Mum bringing out the wobbly tin dish of hot water and kneeling beside him to take off his boots and socks, and saying, "Soak your feet, Sam. Soak them nice and warm again."

That was how she did it when days were cold and wet. Getting home to it made up for being cold. There couldn't have been a better reason in the world for getting home than that. To feel Mum's care, to feel her touch. That was as far as she ever went. Other times when she wanted to tell him she loved him she just smiled.

So once, while she washed his feet, he kissed her in the hair.

"Mum, I reckon you're all right."

"Do you, love?"

"Yeh."

He'd not kissed her in the hair since he was a little boy,

and her arms went up round his neck and she held onto him there. The only time she had hung onto him in years; some idea of hers about cuddling not being the proper training for a manly boy. Strange feeling it turned out to be; the tenderness and strength of her closeness. Like meeting a part of Mum he hadn't known. About a year ago, that must have been. Long, long time ago. It hadn't happened since. Maybe it was best you didn't hammer beautiful things to death. Maybe it was best you let them be. Now she'd say, "Oh, Sam. Eight shillings. You've never brought trouble like this home before."

Well, apart from Rose.

Mum'd do something, though. There never had been a time she couldn't find a way, never a problem she'd not got around.

"Your money feeds you, Sam, and helps keep Pete safely at home. Take that money away and where do we go? Life's very complicated, Sam. Look after your job, love. You're the only job we've got between us. You're our only working man." She'd said something of the kind a few times before.

"When a purse is empty, Sam, any sum of money is a king's ransom. *Anything* is a king's ransom from where I stand." She'd look at him, kind of glazed. (Funny how vivid the imagining was. As if the imagining were real. As if he were looking back upon it, rather than trying to think how it might be. But it was full of bits of things heard at other times.) "Have you stopped to add up," Mum would say, "what eight shillings will buy?"

"Sixty-four *Herald*s, Mum, I reckon. All the *Herald*s you'd ever want to own." Which was a slick and careless thought, or something of the kind.

"Would I allow you to work, love, would I, if we didn't

need the money? If there was any other way, would I allow it? Would I make your studies that much harder for you for any other reason? Why do you think I keep you on at school? Someone in the family has to climb up out of the rut. You're the one, Sam. You're the one with the health and the brains. You've got to stay on long enough to get your certificate, and that'll put you into a bank or the public service and you'll be *safe*. Then one of us will be safe. You've got to have education, Sam, or you'll end up like your father, like the rest of this family, sacked every five minutes when times are tough. You'll be turning bitter and hollow like your dad."

Those bits of paper—were they still there on the road?

No good picking them up: what earthly use are they now? Wet paper. Paper all scattered and driven over. Paper all limp and torn. Who'd sort them into order now? Who'd buy them now? Who'd want them for anything? What butcher or greengrocer would pay me a ha'penny a pound for *them* to wrap things up in? There's nothing in the world you can do with sixty-four soggy newspapers spread wet and spoiled all over the road.

How *can* I go home? After everything that's happened to Mum. Just having Auntie in the house is bad enough. Gawd; that alone is enough to stop every clock in half a mile. Why couldn't that rotten old man have fixed my bike one more time, after all the shillings he's had for fixing it before? He must have made more money out of that bike than the Rothschilds. Now it's gone.

This is what happens to people when they're thinking of ending it all. It is, you know. Well, it must be. Everything falls on top of them and there's no way out from under. You give up, maybe? You give in? And let go? And away you go over the top, over the edge, and what's there? What place do you arrive at then? Is it dark? Is it full of screaming sound? What's it like there? I don't think I want to know in case it's not there at all.

Look, it's only eight shillings. How can eight shillings be the end of the world? But who'd give that kind of money to me and how'd I pay it back? Out of m'tips? What other money do I get? You name it, mate, and it'll be news to me. And I wouldn't get threepence in tips in a week. Take a year. And pay back *who*, I'd like to ask? Who's the millionaire that'd give eight bob to me? And all the cold nights and no potato cakes. Having to pass by that shop with a ha'penny in my pocket, hearing them fry, smelling them fry, smelling them a hundred yards down the road. And having to pass by. . . . I don't mind giving Mum my money as long as I can fiddle a bit on the side for a potato cake. And walking all that way every day, all that way around pulling a billy cart to carry my papers in. And walkin' to school. Walking ten, twelve miles a day. Who'll be paying for the boot leather? I'll be doing it barefoot; I will, you know, *barefoot*. And that's where I draw the line. I've got a bit of pride. Like I said to that old man, if a kid hasn't got his bike he's nothing. And look at it! You couldn't put it together again if you were Merlin the Magician. Fancy falling to bits like that. Heap of rubbish. I'll bet you it was dead cheap in the first place. I'll bet you Grandpa bought it on bargain day, with a couple of spare tires chucked in free.

When I get back to that lousy newspaper shop, what do I say?

"I've lost your *Herald*s, Mr. Lynch."

Can you see me? I mean, can you see me getting away with it?

"Are you trying to pull a George Hogan on me, kid?"

"I've *lost* 'em, Mr. Lynch."

"Conveniently, before you sold any, I bet?"

"Yeh. Yeh. Like you say."

"And lost your moneybag, I bet, and your half-crown in small change?"

"I've *got* my moneybag and I've *got* my small change. Look, I'm not pulling a swiftie. Look, I'm telling you the truth. Would a fellow risk his job for a few lousy papers? All over the place they are. I ran into a tram on Riversdale Road and you don't care at all. I'm lucky I'm not dead. Come and look for yourself if you don't believe."

"Can I leave my shop to go as far as Riversdale Road? You know I can't. And doesn't that suit you fine!"

You can't win with a man like that.

He'll reckon I've sold 'em on the sly. His bloomin' papers are always more important than us kids. Don't do this to *my* papers. Don't do that to them. Don't get 'em wet. Don't tear them. Don't soil them. Don't spoil them. "Delivering my papers in mint condition is what your jobs are about. Start dropping them over fences, start chucking them into gardens, start jamming them into letterboxes and you're *out*, quicker than you can bat an eye."

So he'll be giving me the sack. Bang. Just like he enjoyed it. Which he will.

"I've got thirty kids on the waiting list."

Always holding those kids over us, he is. Or he'll be asking me to pay him back in ten minutes like he did with George.

"Thirty keen kids I've got, waiting on jobs, every one of them busting to start tomorrow. I don't have to mess about with the likes of you."

When George told him he'd lost all that money he just stood there shaking his head. Reckoning the whole thing was put up. Look what he did to George for five shillings and sixpence. Nowhere near as bad as eight shillings. Gawd, he'll hit me; he will, you know. He'll be that blind mad the top'll blow right off his head. Sacked George on the spot and rang up every shop around. "Don't give George Hogan a job if he comes sniffing at your door. He's a liar and a thief." And that was the end of George. And he hasn't written letters to anyone or anythin'. Fourteen years old and gone bush. Sleeping under bridges, they reckon. Going barefoot, they reckon. Or living in a tent made of bags and prospecting for gold somewhere out of Ballarat. No one knows about George, but it's terribly cold up there, they say. All kinds of fellows up there, they say. But you'd think they'd have found him. They couldn't have looked too hard, could they? Or maybe he's gone north instead of west. Up the Murray somewhere. They reckon the sun shines all winter up there. But how do you get to the Murray? It's like a million miles if you haven't got a bike. They say tiger snakes are thick up there, all along the river. Get a bite from one of those and you've had it, mate. I don't reckon I could stand that, worrying about tiger snakes.

"My dad's out of work, Mr. Lynch."

"So your dad's out of work! Who isn't? The way you kids throw my assets around I might as well be out of work myself."

"He's out of work, Mr. Lynch, and so's everyone else at our house. We need the money; we need it like you need air to breathe, Mr. Lynch."

But George didn't get another chance. Everyone at his house was out of work, too. Hadn't made any difference for George. Wouldn't be making any difference for Sam either.

I can't go home; it'll kill 'em. You're riding down the road minding your own business and suddenly nothing's the same anymore. Like you'd forgotten your name or something. Like you'd waked up in a different country or something. The dole money's not going to stretch far enough, is it? That's what Mum's been saying all along—everything's stretched too fine having an extra person in the house, having Pete there and needing special food for him. Lose my bit of paper money, Mum says, and it all falls in a heap. If I go home without my job, it's the end of Pete. It is, you know, the stone end of him. He'll never last a week on his own. It's what Mum's been saying over and over, that it's hard enough and cruel enough for healthy kids getting chucked out of house and home because of laws. Might as well live in the Dark Ages, Mum says. Hard enough for healthy kids having to fight it out on their own, but no kid with diabetes could stand it. Getting wet and cold and sleeping under hedges and not having the proper food. That's what Mum says—if Pete doesn't get the proper food he dies.

When I get home what do I say?

Mum'll have a stroke or something. And Dad'll go and sit in his corner and not look at anyone. And Auntie won't stop nagging for months. Right up that old witch's alley it'll be. And Pete'll say, "It's all right, Mum. You know I should've gone ages ago. You know if they find out I'm not twelve but eighteen the trouble it's going to cause. No more dole for me. Just let me go. Hey?"

Oh gawd.

You'd think for a kid like Pete there'd be some way of bending the rules, so he could stay on home and still get the dole. That's what Mum says—"I don't know, Sam, what these politicians are up to. They say it's government for the people, but it's not government for us, is it?"

Sam hadn't stopped crying because nothing had happened to cheer him up, but he wasn't feeling vague about things now, except the direction he was walking in. He was going especially and particularly nowhere and making a point of it. If there had been a road to the end of the world that's the one he would have taken. If there had been a gate at the end of the road he'd have opened it and stepped through.

He had his bicycle bell in one hand and two shillings and sixpence in small change emptied from his moneybag in the other. The moneybag he had left in the gutter with street water flowing through it. Mr. Lynch owned the moneybag. If he wanted it he could come and get it.

The road Sam had taken was the one to the end of the world, anyway. If you're going to pick it, you'll pick it. Sam had no say in it at all.

Four

BY ABOUT—oh, no one knew what time it was—Sam had developed an ache in his left shoulder as if he had been carrying a heavy weight, as if the socket there had started working loose. It was dark, anyway—black as your hat, as they say—and the ache had settled into a ragged concentration of sharp edges. It always happened when he was tired or cold or his clothes had become too heavy. Sam wasn't built like the strongest fellow in the world, and usually by the end of a hard day he was aching somewhere. Even light clothing became quite heavy then, across the shoulders. Maybe something really was out of place, a bone or something, or it might have been rheumatism. No one knew, least of all Sam, because he hadn't told anyone. What was the point? What could a doctor do about it that he wouldn't charge money for?

Sam had visited a doctor once in his life and that had been for his ears. He had heard Mum say to Dad, "We can't ignore it. You'll have to take him to the doctor. It's too close to his brain."

Going to the doctor in Sam's family meant you were about to be born or were about to die. The pain had been frightful and had got worse after that. I mean, what a dreadful thing to overhear about yourself—that it was too close to your brain! If it was bad enough for the doctor it was probably incurable, like Pete's diabetes, so what point was there in having your worst fears confirmed by running off to the doctor as if he were a fortuneteller who might come up with something a bit less terrible if you crossed his palm with silver? All he could really do was evade your eye and look out the window and mumble something about your having to be brave. "You must face the probability, lad, that in six months you'll be dead."

But it was only wax. About half a yard of it. "Made me real embarrassed," Dad said. "Doesn't that kid ever wash his ears?" It made Sam embarrassed, too. As if going to the doctor and getting away from him alive was a waste of money. As if by dropping dead on the spot everyone would have forgiven him and cheerfully paid the bill. For the florist, as well. You know; for the wreath.

The things a kid thought of! Well, it's part of it, isn't it? All part of the muddle, all part of the pain.

Look, Sam, what are you doing out here? You've got to know. There's got to be a reason.

What a place to be—at this time of night—going the wrong way, not going home, like you had amnesia or something, which you know you haven't got because everything you want to remember you can remember as sharp as a tack. Yeh; what are you up to, Sam? Distant street lights left behind, pale and wet now, showing nothing except that they are there and making cold star patterns in the rain like ports passed by out of reach and never to be known. And across the paddocks, as far out of reach as street lights left behind, small window worlds of yellow light wait for travelers in the dark to come home, but not for Sam. He's a traveler of another kind. It's the dark that's for Sam, a whole night full of it, a forever full of dark.

Is there nothing Mum can do? Nothing left she can sell? Nothing left hidden away that can pay off Lynch and buy an old bike to put him in working order back on the road? Shouldn't he be at home right now baking beside that fire thawing the ice out of his bones? Leaning on Mum one more time. "Help me, Mum; one more time. Tell me what to do, Mum; one more time." But there comes a time, kid, there comes another kind of time in the affairs of a man.

A thing that's *going*, Sam, is supposed to know where it's going. Like a tramcar on rails. There's the name stuck up front for all to see, City, or Spencer Street, or Wattle Park, or whatever, and it sets out businesslike and gets there. Well, with any sort of luck it gets there as long as it doesn't go hitting too many stupid kids on the way. So what about you? Do you keep on going hoping there'll be another day waiting for you out here in the dark somewhere? A day that's going to come up bright and clear and sensible. How far away is it going to be? A very long time, Sam, from the look of it from here. Tuesday's light has barely gone and Wednesday's can't be ready yet. All night long Wednesday will be lying low out here in this great mass of darkness working itself up into a frenzy until it's ready to happen. What if you miss it, Sam?

What if Wednesday lies near the edge somewhere and you

start going in a circle (the way lost people are said to do) and miss the edge? Does the dark go on then, and on, and on? I mean, there are mysteries, aren't there? The world's not straightforward. Strange things happen that are not imagined.

"Where are you, Sam?" Mum must be saying. "What have you done, Sam?" she must be saying. "For heaven's sake, why aren't you home yet? It's so late."

Someone will come knocking on the door; Lynch, probably. Lynch looking at Mum as if it's all her fault; Mum shrinking into a tight knot of fright.

"I don't know what he's done with himself, Mrs. Collins," Lynch'll say. "I'm not here to discuss the state of his health. That's your business, Mrs. Collins. My business is papers, papers not delivered. Eight shillings' worth of papers to be recovered. Two shillings and sixpence in small change to be accounted for. That boy turns out to be a common thief like the Hogan kid, Mrs. Collins. So what do we do?"

WANTED

FOR THE DESTRUCTION OF 64 *Herald*s
AND THE INFAMOUS THEFT OF
TWO SHILLINGS AND SIXPENCE

SAMUEL SPENCER COLLINS

AGED 14 YEARS. HEIGHT 5 FEET 8 INCHES.
WEIGHT 112 POUNDS. BROWN HAIR. GRAY EYES.
PALE COMPLEXION. SCAR ON LEFT CHEEK.
(FROM SITTING WHEN SEVEN ON A SOLDERING IRON)

SHOOT ON SIGHT

UPON DELIVERY OF SCALP TO POLICE HQ,
A BOUNTY OF TWO SHILLINGS WILL BE PAID.

But worrying about what might be happening back there had as much point as worrying about great dobs of wax in his ears of a year ago. Or about the ache in his shoulder. Or about anything, if it came to that. Why hadn't he gone to a railway station and got on a train? On a train with windows shut and doors shut and glass all steamed up inside with hot breath, the miles outside rushing by unseen, not hurting a bit, rushing by so fast without any pain, *getting* him somewhere.

Wasn't it the obvious thing to do? To get on a train and go? He must have been born stupid. With two shillings and sixpence to spend he could have gone from here to evermore, to Ballarat, or Bendigo, or Bairnsdale, a hundred or two hundred miles from here; unimaginable distances when you've lived at 14 Wickham Street for fourteen years and gone nowhere that you couldn't reach on foot or by bicycle in half a day. Maybe a smart kid could get away with it for less, maybe for no money at all, by hiding under a seat or hanging on somewhere, but saving on the fare wasn't always the smartest thing around. A kid had to be crazy though, just crazy, to head for the bush this way, with an empty belly, with rain and dark lying all around like there'd never been a beginning to the world, as if God had never said, "Let there be light."

That's how it was. Truly it was. Like groping out toward the edge wondering if the edge was getting close or was still a long way away, wondering whether you were about to fall off, wondering if there was an edge at all between the possible and the impossible.

A shape was there somewhere and it felt like a church. There's a feeling for such occasions. You know? A presence, an awareness of bulk, of a building brooding. And what else but a church would stand alone out there in 1931? Nothing but a church would dare. There was a hedge, or something of the kind with prickles not sharp enough to tear, and a wire fence with a gate that Sam found under his hands, a gate that he opened and a path that he walked on and a porch that he came to, a porch with three solid faces like a solid mass of wood, each face standing square to the rain no matter which way Sam turned. Rain blowing three ways and no fourth way to go, except inside to get away from it all. From inside a faint red glow touched the high curve of a window arch; so very faint, the glow, that it was hardly there.

Get inside, Sam, and the rain may fall and the wind may blow just any way they please all night through. Get in there and stop worrying about Wednesday lying a thousand years away. Sleeping in there, safe and warm and dry, and a thousand years will be barely a moment before you open your eyes. That's true, too. How do you know? About sleep, I mean, about waking up on the other side of it? You've got to take it on trust; just shut your eyes and forget all about it and hope that tomorrow will be the proper tomorrow, not August 12 a thousand years away.

So why does God lock the door?

Solid, solid, locked.

"Can't You feel my shoulder here? Can't You feel me pushing here? It's me. It's Sam. From Lipcott Street Methodists', the old stone church, the one that's been there sixty years. And I always say my prayers and never miss a Sunday—You know that Auntie sees to that like she had a personal directive with the Holy Seal stamped upon it. Or won't You open up because I've stolen half a crown? Or does the Catholic God live here on the other side of this door? Well, you never know, do you; the things they say. Maybe it's different."

Hardwood planks, battened and bolted through, swollen

wet and thick and tight and insensitive to Sam from weeks of rain.

"Please, God, open Your door. Just for tonight. In the morning I'll catch a train and go away and not trouble You any more."

Two front doors and two side doors and two back doors, all six doors locked or padlocked against Sam. Different in the olden days, they say. Even in the Dark Ages that Mum talks about. Churches were places of refuge then, even for thugs and thieves and runaways.

At the back, below floor level, Sam found something that felt like a hole. He wasn't sure how he managed to come upon it or what purpose it served. Perhaps cats made it or dogs made it or God quickly put it there. Sam explored with an arm and poked his head through and squeezed the rest of himself in after, having to push desperately hard. Inside, under the floorboards of the church, was a densely black but spacious dry place and he curled into a ball on his left side. By pressing his shoulder into the earth the ache soon went away.

They had Evening Fellowship there that night. They had been having it on Tuesdays in that building for something like thirty years, and went on having it for another thirty or so until they built that peculiar modern thing around 1967 and jacked the old place up off its foundations and sold it, termites and all, for carting away. A few minutes after the building had gone, a kid fossicking through the dust where the vestry used to be found eighteen pence in old money and a rusted-up bicycle bell that wouldn't ring. He bought a Coke and a peanut bar with the eighteen pence and threw the bell into a vacant lot on the way home.

Sam didn't hear the people at their meeting, which lasted

for forty-five minutes. Nor did he hear them in the vestry afterward, above his head, where they had tea and biscuits and gossiped as usual until half-past nine. I suppose if he had heard, the course of his life would have gone another way.

Five

SAM BECAME aware of a hot spot in the middle of his chest and of another in his shoulder blades—a reluctant awareness of a foreign influence creeping into his consciousness from a great distance off, as if in the middle of an enormously important journey, across a vast tract of time, someone was calling on him to abandon the journey before his time was up. So the spots, as he resisted them, were sometimes close and sometimes remote, but they then became part of a dream in which Auntie slapped scalding hot poultices on to him to draw the evil out of his body. This was such an appalling idea, even in the depths of sleep, that he woke up yelling, "Here, you lay off. You leave me alone. Stick the flipping poultices on yourself."

Auntie wasn't there and the poultices were frightened cats hissing, scattering into the gloom away from Sam's sudden and savage attack, leaving Sam almost as startled himself and giddily disoriented.

He sighed then out of an immediate pit of despondency, such a pit, oh such a pit it was.

Talk about the edge of the world! He had been dithering at the brink of it all right, and now it was tipping him off, into an even deeper pit, and he dug his fingers frantically into dirt and dust and a patch of mud to hold on to what he had, though none of it for the moment was comprehensible.

None of it looked like the sort of thing a fellow should have had to live with first thing in the morning—a few slits of weak gray light and vague heaps of earth or rubbish, and posts standing up like mushroom stalks upon which a deep blackness bore heavily down, and everything else disappearing darkly into the earth at unnatural angles. Oh my goodness, it was eerie. No bed. No canvas flapping. No insurance-company calendar with a map of the world on it to tick off the day. No worn comics (on the bentwood chair) carefully read by nineteen boys before they reached Sam. No call from the kitchen either.

"Come on, Sam. Oh, do come on, Sam, or you'll be late for school."

"What's for breakfast, Mum?"

"Sausage meat and potato, love, but get yourself out of there or you'll not have time to eat a thing."

None of that. Maybe none of it forevermore. Yeh; he had run away as millions of teenage boys over thousands of years had run away before him. And Wednesday had come. Well, something had come. He had crossed the Styx, or whatever you called it, and found daylight again. So it could have been worse.

Today was the day for the train. Today he would *go*, and the idea wasn't all that awful.

Go where? Gee whiz. Go where? A hundred miles maybe. There was real excitement in the thought of that.

No school today (or tomorrow), no French, no gruesome trigonometry, no homework, no Auntie (hallelujah), no Lynch and his lousy newspapers, no bike either. . . . What about Mum and Dad? Yeh, what about Pete?

Was it time for counting up things lost and things gained, or was it time for a bit of blind panic?

It was distinctly cold where the hot spots had been. That had been a cozy little cuddle. Yes indeed. That had been very good. Fancy making a fuss big enough to scare them away. Cuddles were nice. Oh yes. Cuddling up to living things. Oh, cuddling up to a real live girl. Wouldn't that be something?

"Here, puss," Sam crooned. "Here kitty, kitty, kitty. Come on back and have another cuddle."

It was surprising how dry he felt and how generally warm, everything considered. How long had he slept, for pity's sake? Long enough to dry out his clothes with body heat? That'd be just *marvelous* for his rheumatism, as the women at home would have told him. But there weren't any aches for the moment, except the great big empty one in his belly, and that was murder. Could he buy a pie or something? He'd eaten almost nothing since breakfast yesterday. It was true, you know. A lovely juicy meat pie with tomato sauce. How about that? Did they make potato cakes at this time of day? If it came to that, what day was it?—his clothes being dry and all! Maybe he had slept a week surrounded by hot cats?

If the cats were angry would they scratch his eyes out? Cats skulking in the dark. They *were* cats, of course. Well, they'd have to be! What else, for heaven's sake?

"Here kitty, kitty, kitty," Sam said nervously, as if offering big saucers of fresh creamy milk and lifelong love, hoping they were not life-size tigers. "I'm not going to eat you."

Cat pie?

With tomato sauce?

Urk.

Someone mewed at his left and someone else mewed behind him and two scrawny young animals barely out of kittenhood, one apparently yellow, the other apparently black, separated from the darkness and rubbed against him, all warm and wriggling and purring, to accept the cautious blessing of his hands.

"If you promise not to scratch me," Sam said, sighing a bit, "I'll promise, absolutely, not to eat you."

It could have been worse. Imagine waking up with tiger snakes down your neck! Having a cuddle with a tiger snake would be just about the end.

Yeh.

Magpies were out there in the day—their conversation as easily identified as the purring of the cats. They made the day sound pretty good. There was a thrush at a distance; well, probably a thrush—Sam was not the world authority on birds. If it crowed he knew it was a rooster. If it said "pretty Polly" and ate nuts it had to be a parrot. If it yodeled it was sure to be a magpie. If it sang very nicely it was a thrush—or Ernie Scarlett of Wickham Street, who could imitate anything. But it couldn't be Ernie this morning unless he was in very strong voice, because he lived so far away. Several dogs were screaming abuse at each other across half a mile and an extremely self-important pigeon strutted and cooed very close by, on top of the church most likely. Practically bursting his puffed-up shirt front by the sound of it, showing off in front of a lady pigeon. Pigeons were worse than people when it came to woo. Well, almost. An awful lot of wooing must go on somewhere—look at all the people in the world. Waiting for it, you know, just waiting for things to start was like waiting for a train that never came. Looking into the distance along the line. Nothing ever there.

Well, an awful lot of other things were going on out there,

one way and another, though Sam could scarcely say he was
blinded by the brilliant light of day or deafened by the sound
of human activity either: out there it seemed to be a world
inhabited by other species, which might have indicated that it
was safe for a fellow to go out into it, unless the dogs were
bloodhounds with Mr. Lynch hanging on the end of them!
The Hounds of Lynchville! Well, why not? No kid who
worked for him would have put it past him!

"What do you reckon, puss-cats?"

Sam groped round for his overcoat—it still felt as wet as
when he had discarded it some time during the night—and
crawled with it back to the hole, the hole that had started
looking far too small to be real. There had to be a mistake,
or another hole, because he'd have needed to be pretty desperate to have got in through there, or maybe he'd got in
because he'd not seen it. What you don't get a proper look at,
you don't worry about so much. As for getting out of it?

Sam pushed his coat through and edged his head up into
the gray day to find himself against the lip of a concrete
path. What was *that* doing there? So hard and so permanent
and so inconveniently placed.

"Hey," said Sam.

He pulled back for a few moments and tried a second
time, leading with one arm and then with both arms to protect his head. Something didn't seem to be right, but how
could it be anything other than right? I mean, it was crazy.

"Oh, come off it, Sam," he said to himself, "you got in,
you've got to be able to get out; it's elementary mathematics." So by dint of twisting and wriggling he forced himself
a fraction farther, but it was an uncommonly anxious experience, as if by struggling harder he was making it worse.
And that gave him a strange view of the world, the edge of

the path looking like the Great Wall of China, the back of the church looking as if it were about to fall on top of him, and swaying pine trees looking unstable and menacing and higher than the sky. A very strange-looking world it was he had got himself into. Maybe he should have come out from under another way, on his back, perhaps, rather than on his chest. That might have given him more twist. Then he'd have been able to get his shoulders back in again, or completely out, one way or the other.

The angles for squeezing down that hole and for squeezing up out again seemed to be dramatically *not the same*, and Sam's pulse was beating faster from trying not to get too scared about it, from trying not to think about it at all, and from trying to forget that all those abrasions he collected under the tram felt like they were about to start bleeding again, just to be difficult. Yeh, *and* from thinking that from where he was lying going up through the S bend of a sewer pipe might have been dead easy by comparison.

Who's going to find you, Sam, and when are they going to find you, if you don't get out of here soon? On Saturday, maybe, when the ladies arrive to pretty up the church for Sunday? They can put the flowers round you, Sam, instead of in the vases. They can place them at your head and feet. Are you going to be stuck here until you're dead? Samuel Spencer Collins, deceased, unexpectedly, due to his being fourteen years and four months. If he'd been thirteen he'd have got through the blasted hole with inches to spare. That's the trouble: not being used to how big you are. You shoot up like a beanstalk overnight and don't notice and no one bothers to tell you.

Maybe you should start to hallo. And then what? Some-one brings a shovel to dig you out of the ground, or a

saw to cut you out of the wall, or a chisel to chip you out
of the concrete, or the fire brigade in all its splendor comes
clanging down the street to flush you out with a hose (oh
my gawd), and all the sticky-beaking world comes running
madly after. That is, if anyone hears you at all.

Where are the houses, Sam? Where are all the people? You
know, like men on the way to work and kids on the way
to school, all the people who'd be hearing you if you started
yelling. You headed in the wrong direction, kid, that's the
way it looks, and walked right off the edge of the city of
Melbourne. But if you do stir somebody up, what happens
then? Maybe Lynch turns up. Maybe Mum turns up. And the
mess starts getting messier. Remember, Sam, you're *going*.
On your blooming own. Solo. Like Hinkler in his little airplane. Today's the day for going, you don't know where, but
you're going.

He screwed the toes of his boots into the earth behind
him and practically twisted his arms inside out against the
church and started *pushing*, but he couldn't raise his shoulders
high enough. The bending was the trouble—there wasn't
enough bend in him, couldn't bend along the wall or up and
over that towering path. All he managed to do was force
himself harder against the concrete like some dimwitted
chicken growing bigger and bigger inside an egg and not
having the sense to peck his way out of it. And that was
worse than ever; much, much worse than ever.

"Oh, gee."

He gave up then; what point was there in going on? And
he panted across the few uneasy minutes that lay between
exhaustion and the beginnings of an awful idea, no half-baked
or fleeting fancy, a real and deadly earnest idea that he feared
to follow through, but that took him darkly on its way to its

inevitable ending. He might as well have been in his coffin with the lid nailed down! So a cat padded sensuously across the path at eye level. There it went, padding across the path in front of Sam's eyes, looking about five feet high, and started rolling on its back as friendly as you like a few feet away, as if it had come home again, as if that slab of concrete was as soft as clover. Were there two cats the same? Scrawny and young and about as yellow as a cat could be? One under the church, scratching round, trying to find its way out past Sam—and another in the open here? Not likely. Couldn't feel anyone scratching round back there. No cat at all; not of any color.

It wasn't the same hole, was it? Sam had come squeezing through the wrong one, hadn't he? It couldn't be done, a mistake as stupid as that, but he had done it, easier than spelling his name out loud. How could anyone be so dumb?

Easy, mate. I don't even have to try. Like Auntie says, the boy's got brains he's never used.

"Help. Oh, help me."

No one came.

"Please help me. I know it's silly, *but I'm stuck here,* I really am."

How do things like this happen? You know? Suddenly a fellow's in it and what does he do? How does he turn back time and come at it for a second go?

All his stars must have set or something. All those lucky stars—where were they? All those guardian angels—where had they gone? And what about God up there, sitting on His cloud?

"Can't anybody hear me? Isn't anybody there? Here I am. Under the church. Someone's got to get me out of here."

But if anyone was around they must have been indoors

making lots of noise eating celery or playing Gramophones, and he was half-buried, anyway, and probably muffled, and there were magpies and thrushes and wind in the pines and the thousand sounds of day.

What had gone wrong in the world? Everything was out of balance, all order was disturbed. It was as if Death was determined to get him, and brooked no change. As if his time was up. As if he'd been meant to die under that flaming tram and getting out of it alive had been a mistake in the Divine Plan.

"Please. Please hear me."

I'm only fourteen.

Look, that's not old enough to die. What about all the things I want to do? What about kissing Rose? What about exploring Egypt and the Pharaohs' tombs? What about winning my race next Picnic Day? What about flying an airplane nonstop across the Poles?

Lying there like that, just like waiting for the end to happen, as if you couldn't stop it, *as if you had no say*.

Like lying on your bed in the hours when the spirit is low and life is immense; lying there alone in the blackout, so dark, so dense, the spirit so tiny in the deep and silent night, thinking of German Focke-Wulf 190's out where the Atlantic is gray and blue, out where clouds in days of grayness scud along the ocean like rain through pines when you're fourteen. Like lying under that church when you were fourteen. So long ago.

So then you were a boy with a man's job to do. Growing up if you're a boy is a man's job at any time. But dying's the job for now and that's just got to be the job for a full-grown man. And German Focke-Wulf 190's are all about dying (even if you're German). I mean, what else could they make them for and for what other use? All that power. All those guns. Only enough room inside for a fellow to fly them and shoot the guns. So they make them for killing, that's all. For killing you, boy, because you speak a different language and sing a different tune when the national anthem plays. Name me one more thing they make Focke-Wulf 190's for and I'll pay you the prize.

Well, lying on your own at night except for Johnny over there, Flying Officer Johnny Speight, aged 22, on the other bed, Johnny from Sydney twelve thousand miles away, Johnny lying there stupefied by alcohol (an escape for Johnny who doesn't have to fly with his hands, but never an escape for you, Sam; eleven lives and a flying boat in your hands), Johnny terrified but made dull, gentle Johnny on his back snoring like a fat middle-aged man (that's the kind of belly he'll get if he doesn't give the beer away—soft, billowing belly in twenty more years, if he doesn't die tomorrow or today), Johnny lying there snoring offensively, forgetting all those cannons in the sky searching for you, all those cannon eyes, all those cannon muzzles in airplane wings, all those cannon shells with names written on them: this one for John Speight, navigator; this one for Robert Sydney Lyons, air gunner; this one for Bryan Howard Fairbairn, flight engineer; this one for Malcolm McGlasham, second pilot; which one for Samuel Spencer Collins, captain? Each shell with a name written on it. Some miss, I'm happy to say.

Oh, yes, lying there night by night (is it June, is it May, is it 1941 or 1942?). Whose German mother's son will be pressing the little black button to fire the gun to shoot the shell to blow your head off and far away? Which kid from Hamburg, hair like flax, eyes of blue, is going to get you,

Sam? Who's going to smear you all over the bulkhead wall like a bucket of goo?

Or will you be blowing his head off, Sam?

Will you be mesmerizing him, boy, turning your airplane so steeply near the water that he can't match your turn, that he goes straight in concentrating on gun-sight images, caught in the magnetism of your tightening turn, exploding in with fire and spray, smearing himself into a pretty sheen of oil to calm the sea for now and to catch the sunrise with spectrum colors next time the clouds have gone? Yeh, why should poor old Mum get all the bad news? Time for some other Mum to take her turn, that being the shape of life around this here niche of time. What about Pete? What about Dad? What about Sam? My Mum, left living with Auntie. Oh my gawd, how's *that* for bad news? But isn't that the story of the world—the wrong people winning all the time?

Lying there, counting up the bodies that melt away, counting up the coffins, counting up the aircraft that don't come home from patrol. What coffins? Long airplanes for long kids; they're the only coffins they give you out there. Buried with full military honors, but no brass band. A real nice funeral pyre to burn up the remains, no expense spared, unless you smash into the ocean before you're desiccated by flames. The sharks can have you then, or some other carrion-eater of the seas. Way down deep. Oh, way down. Where it's night forever and you drift in limbo like a ribbon of kelp, or something comes along that has a taste for bone. Beautiful prime young bone, all those loving years growing in the garden.

Oh, my darling.

Lying on that bed at night, aching from spirit tiredness,

and body tiredness, and loneliness for her. Some don't care
—they don't, you know. Maybe they're the lucky ones. They
love her and leave her until they go back another time, but
not Sam. Sam goes on being empty for her when she's not
there. Lonely all the time. What a fate for a boy twelve
thousand miles from home, being a one-woman man; the
world full of beautiful girls all half-crazy to love a man
because of war, Sam wanting only her and she's not there.

Lying waiting for the opening of the door, for the click
of the light switch, for the Duty Officer to say, "Two o'clock
in the morning, Sam. Time for another day."

As if anyone would want to know at that hour; as if you'd
been praying for it to start happening. Well, maybe that's
the way. Get it done. Get it over with. *But somehow you've
got to stay alive to get back home. Back home to there.
Back home to her.*

"Aircrew Mess in half an hour," the Duty Officer says.
"Briefing at 0300. The weather looks O.K." And somehow
you bring a few sparks of consciousness to bear on the call,
somehow you force life from heaven knows where back into
the body that's afraid to be awake, that's afraid to die; somehow you force it to start making the moves that take it out
to play the big hero one more time. The last time?
Who knows?

The flying-boat captain. The poised young pilot. The
straight back. The square smile.

Yeh, the big hero one more time; the first time, the second
time, the thirtieth time, now the forty-seventh time you lay
your life on the line. Always one more. Always more to go.
So you live today. So you get back alive. What about
tomorrow? The forty-seventh time.

You never finish under sixty-five or seventy times. You

need that many to make up your eight hundred hours on operational patrol that they graciously call an operational tour, one boy's war effort in Coastal Command.

Coastal Command, for God's sake; and half the time land is a thousand miles astern.

Yeh. Sixty-five times, unless you start shaking in a corner, unless you start biting your nails *all* the time, unless they catch you in a quiet place on your own with tears in your eyes.

"What's wrong with you son, eh?" And you shake uncontrollably and cannot say.

Admit to fear? Admit to being afraid? *Tell* them that you're terrified when your whole life has been directed toward the attainment of man-sized courage and man-sized nerve? "Be a man," Auntie used to say when you were eight years of age. "Don't snivel, boy."

"Square your shoulders, son," Mum used to say, "and make me proud."

"Take it on the chin, Sam," Dad used to say before he got T.B. and died. "Even when you're down, never let 'em know or they'll flay you alive. You can't win against them, boy."

"Greater love hath no man than this," the parson used to say, "that a man lay down his life for his friends. . . . Let us always be aware of the freedom we inherit from the love of the glorious heroes who so gladly died."

Gladly died?

Heroes must have changed.

"For God," the parson used to say on Armistice Day when Sam was a boy, and on Anzac Day and on every other day when it crossed his mind, "for the King, for love, and for the honor of our glorious dead we, too, are prepared to lay down our lives."

The Duty Officer. Still there. "Johnny must be dead, I think. I can't wake him, Sam, though he seems to be breathing. Maybe it's reflexes still twitching from a lifetime of grog and degradation. He wasn't hitting it last night, was he? Kick him in the ribs, will you? Stir him out."

"Yeh."

And each time you wake up Johnny, each time he navigates you down into the Bay of Biscay, are you waking him up for the last time? Wake up, Johnny. Wake up, Johnny. Wake up and die. Johnny's got that look about him, you know? So beautiful, so out of this world, that he'll never make old bones. The gods take his kind back again as soon as they can arrange the day.

It's a problem flying with Johnny. If the gods take back Johnny, are they going to be so particular that they'll not take back you?

Or is it the other way around?

"Sam," she says, in every letter to him, every day. "You're beautiful. You're the one. You're my man."

"Wake up, Johnny. Come on. Oh, wake up, Johnny Speight. It's time to fly."

Or we'll not be there when it's time to die.

"Can't you hear me, anybody? Can't you hear me here? Under the church. Is it the cemetery or something? Isn't anyone alive?"

Stuck, you know, like some stupid little kid sticking his finger up a water tap, then someone's got to come and cut the tap away.

Oh gawd, who's going to come to cut the church away?

After a while the yellow cat was within reach and Sam cuddled it in his arms.

"You're a nice puss," he said. "Will you come with me when I go on the train?"

Later Sam said, "You're so skinny. You're skinnier than me, I reckon. Maybe it's not the wrong hole at all. I reckon you could've squeezed out through a crack in the wall."

Then Sam said, "Don't you ever eat? Doesn't anyone give you a feed? Did you leave home like me or get chucked out on your ear? I suppose you're a lady cat having kittens all the time and they can't be bothered with you any more. Are all the mice eaten up? Are you too slow to catch a bird? Or did you go away from your mother before you learned? You can belong to me if you like, but don't go having kittens, will you? I couldn't stand that. We'd never be able to carry them around."

In about an hour it was raining heavily, beating in from the side, and Sam managed to arrange his overcoat to break the worst of it for a while. The cat seemed content to stay until water started spilling over the roof gutters, blocked by pine needles probably, and came pouring down the wall and turned the narrow gap between the path and the building into a drain. Lying in a drain running with water wasn't the best place to be at any time, particularly if you didn't need to be there. The cat started struggling and crying and digging in her claws and Sam had to let her go. She simply ran off, angry and bristling, ran in a moment out of his vision and was gone. Sam was wet by then and started screaming for help, while rain thundering on the corrugated iron roof and water spilling to the ground were making sounds like the end of the world.

"Oh gawd," Sam cried, "I'm going to drown."

He fought like fury, as he had fought that boy behind the incinerator, *ferociously*, and something inside his body seemed to move to make way for other things. The earth around him was turning to mud, was turning soft like potter's clay, and out came Sam, out he came sliding free, frantic tears on his cheeks streaming with mud in the rain, and to get away from there was all he wanted to do. Who could say that horrible hole would not try to suck him back in again? Rain pouring down, blood spreading from his hips and knees, fear like sparks of fire exploding to the tips of his fingers and toes. "Oh gawd," he sobbed, and ran with desperation for the road, sprawling with an ungainly stride round the side of the building, his way to the gate interrupted by a girl holding a large black umbrella.

Sam groaned, but a great and painful tension in him almost at once went away. He saw her instantly and clearly as if he had known her all his life and had expected her to be waiting where she stood, water spilling from her umbrella like strings of beads to the ground.

Six

SHE WORE an outsize overcoat, perhaps a man's castoff, hanging very low with a wet and bedraggled hem, no hat, and drabness. Her features were small and sharp, and very good to look at. Her hair—oh, her hair, so long and straight and fine, and soft enough, despite the weather, to bloom in the wind. That was how her hair seemed to be, independently alive, blooming upward into the dark cone of the ribs of the umbrella, into an inner gloom there that belonged to dreams rather than to the light of day.

It was all so strange, but so important. Yes, Sam; so important. Yes, Sam. . . .

It was as if she had been waiting for years for this moment to arrive, waiting right here, as perhaps he had been preparing all life long for the moment of floundering along the church wall to confront her, so suddenly, so completely, as if everything that had ever happened to him had been part of getting ready for now. For what other reason would the world dare to stop turning round? For a long moment it did, it did just that—the whole world fell silent and became still and its violence paused.

He saw her speak before he heard any voice. From the movement of her lips there came no sound, but all at once there were words, all mixed up with an assault of wind and rain as if her question had traveled across years through storm on the way.

"Have you been yelling? Are you the one?"

That was not what he had expected. There should have been something like, "Doctor Livingstone, I presume." He had forgotten all about being stuck back there, but back it came, all the fright and the fear, and he nodded, trying not to show too clumsily how disturbed he was. But it was hard, awfully hard; struggling into his overcoat, such a muddy mess it was, but struggling into it to give himself something to do. Oh, a grown-up girl and so pretty, and old enough to kiss a fellow and not bat an eye. Old enough not to run away or tell her mum. But he was always so clumsy with girls, even with little girls. Always said the wrong things to them. Always made the wrong moves, even with Rose, and Rose was only thirteen. Only thirteen even now.

Rose—ah, Rose—riding on the crossbar of his bicycle; first

time ever that she sat there. Only time, if it came to that. All the other times were imaginings. So light she was a strong wind might have blown her off. (When they're fragile like that—oh, when they're fragile like Rose, your heart swells up.)

I'll not be letting the wind blow you off, Rose. Nothing will hurt you while I'm looking after you. Oh, you're safe with me, Rose. Oh, you bet.

"Will you really come with me, Rose?"

"Yeh."

"Blackberry picking, out past Mont Albert School—away out there, just the two of us?"

"Yeh."

"Today?"

"Yeh."

(Yow-eeeee! But she hadn't heard the cheer—that was locked away inside—though maybe a bit of it showed. Hard to know what you felt. One minute it's all so wild; but in a moment, so tender, so confused. Dear Rose.)

Gee, I love having you there, double-dinking on my bike with me, my arms reaching around you to the handlebars, touching you in a way, but not *deliberately*. Not being fresh, just making you safe in there, all wrapped up. A fellow's got to hold the handlebars; the bike won't steer on its own. You've got to balance the thing, or you end up in a heap on the road. But your mum'll be mad if she finds out. Gawd, don't you tell her, Rose. My life won't be worth living if they hear a breath of it at home. I mean, we're not supposed to be together, are we, alone and all that, and it's dangerous, they say, awfully dangerous to go double-dinking on a bike out on the road where the traffic goes.

"Watch your dress, Rose."

"Yeh."

"Keep the hem tight, Rose. Keep it tucked up. If it gets caught in the wheel, if we fall off, if we get hurt, they'll find out then; then they'll know."

Rose knows that. Oh yes, she knows. Rose is not so vacant she doesn't understand.

Darting off down back streets before anyone sees us go. Don't want kids seeing either, because they tease, and there are kids like Herbie Mann who'd run a mile to tell a tale. Strange kid he is. What makes him tick? The world's full of them, Sam; full of the odd ones; oh yes, mate.

Rose balancing on the bar, kind of sidesaddle, toes pointing so gracefully (they ought to send her to ballet school, though who would pay?), Rose poised there between his arms, her long brown plaits swinging like long brown cords; then bike and boy and girl sweeping away down Union Road. No one will see us now.

"I saw your Rose double-dinking with Sam Collins, Mrs. Vaughan."

"Did you now! Where?"

"Down Union Road, Mrs. Vaughan. Going somewhere, they were. He was awfully close to her."

"I'll flay that boy."

"Yes, Mrs. Vaughan. I thought you'd want to know."

Riding two and a half miles with Rose—well, riding along the flat parts and on the downgrades; walking with her where the country takes an uphill turn, but saying hardly a word. Well, when a girl's not eleven yet and a fellow's just twelve, there's not much you can say. I mean, you can't tell her you think she's beautiful, that you love sneaking looks at her all the time, that you love brushing against her just any old way, and to catch her eye sends you up through the clouds—you can't blurt that sort of thing out cold. It's so soppy and it's not really allowed. What if you said it, and she told someone, and kids started teasing you, and the mums heard, *what would you say?* But she's there, at your side, running on foot the two of you, bicycle bouncing away from the road. Sam, you've made it; you're alone with a girl, not a person in sight, not a house—if you run the right way.

Skylarks out here, above the paddocks. Magpies in the trees. Dry grass on the high lands, dusty thickets of blackberries along the gullies. Keep an eye peeled, Sam. You're looking after her now. You're caring for her, Sam. There could be snakes out here.

Standing with Rose, getting your breath back, a hot flush of sweat breaking out all over, Rose always looking another way.

"What are we going to put the blackberries in, Sam? We didn't bring a bag."

"We could eat 'em, Rose."

"They're green, Sam."

"They shouldn't be. The kids reckoned they were ripe long ago."

"They're green, Sam."

"Let's do something else then?"

"What, Sam?"

"We could sit down and have a rest for a while."

Sitting on the hillside with Rose, flicking at the bike to make the front wheel turn round, to make the sun shine on the spokes as if a bubble's sheen lay within the rim, Rose looking at the ground most of the time.

"I'm thirsty, Sam. Did you bring some water?"

"No."

"Have you got any chewie?"

"No."

"I'm thirsty."

"Swallow some spit, Rose."

He should have thought of that, should have thought of water; should have brought a bag, too. Forgetting those things wasn't caring properly for Rose. I mean, if anyone asked, how were they to explain? "Picking blackberries? Were you indeed? Did you get enough for a pie? Show me your fingers. Don't see any stains." Grownups never believe. I wonder why.

Sam feeling so strange. Yeh, so strange; as if he had left part of himself somewhere else and not all of him had arrived—the part up top that did the thinking. It was a funny dead-head kind of feeling, though he knew what to say, just the same.

"Rose."

"Yeh."

"Would you undo your plaits so I could see your hair fall down?"

"What do you want to see my hair for?"

He couldn't tell her because he didn't know.

They sat in the open with the sun on their heads, and the skylarks sang above them and dropped like feathered stones and the magpies sang as if the world were their own and the grass was as dry and as hard as little sticks and there was a sneezy smell of hot dry earth and the dust of straw.

In a while her hands went up and her plaits came down and her hair fell shining and long and free with lights in it you couldn't see at other times. He wished he could put his face to it and feel the freshness there, but she was too far away. Oh, it was lovely, so lovely, her hair. It would have to feel clean and cool, wouldn't it, looking like that. Like sweet

cotton sheets it would be, just laundered, pressed to your
face while you breathed.

"Rose."

"Yeh."

"Can I kiss you now?"

Oh, there was a change, a sudden change that he couldn't
understand and couldn't explain. Oh, a feeling that she had
suddenly gone away.

"What do you want to kiss me for?" Such a flat little
voice it was, so much smaller than before.

"I just want to."

"Why?"

"Because boys always want to kiss girls. You knew, didn't
you? You knew that's what we'd do when you came."

"You said we'd pick blackberries, but the blackberries are
green."

"Ah, go on, Rose. Give me a kiss. It's not going to hurt
you. It's not like getting a tooth out or anything. No one
can see. We're all on our own."

"I don't want to play kisses. I want to go home."

"Please, Rose. Just a kiss. Just one. Just one for the first
time. It'll be nice."

"I want to go home. I don't like kissing games."

"Gee, Rose."

But she ran. Up she leaped and off she ran, over the brow
of the hill and into the gorse. Gorse bushes everywhere.
Where was Rose? Not a sign.

"Rose!"

Disappeared—as if she had not been with him, as if she had
never been there at all.

He must have walked a mile, or two miles, or four, here
and there, up and down, round and round, dragging that

stupid bike through gullies and ditches and grass like knives, with an aching, crying dullness inside, afraid even to put the bike down in case he couldn't find it again.

"Rose! You must have known. You must have known I didn't mean blackberries. Gee, you must have known it was a kissing game."

Running backward and forward to the road—never anyone that looked like Rose. She could have hidden anywhere, could have fallen down a hole, could have been bitten by a snake, or been spirited away. How could she go? Was it to be a mystery—Rose, never to be found? And he had been *caring* for her. In Sam's care, and she had gone.

"Rose. Don't hide any more. Come on out, Rose, and let's go home. Rose, you've got to show yourself, please. It's not fair. You'll get me into trouble, Rose."

Everybody would be in it. Search parties and dogs and torches at night on the hillside. People yelling, "Where are you, little girl?" Everybody would know.

Going home.

It must have been late because the sun was low. Oh, what would he say? Oh, Rose, I'm so sad for you; I'm so sorry, Rose, making you run away. Gee, Mrs. Vaughan, I looked everywhere for Rose. Look at me, all scratched and torn; look at my clothes. Gee, Mum—oh, gee, Mum, I don't know what to say.

Going home. Oh, what a day.

Wickham Street looking just the same. How could it, you know? As if it didn't care. Poor Rose gone, but the street looking just the same.

"Sam Collins, come here!"

Enough to stop a fellow's heart. Such a bellow it was. Everyone in a mile must have heard.

Rose's dad—oh gee, her dad—striding down his front path just like he's going to kill you, Sam.

"What have you been doing with Rose?"

Sam straddling his bike in the middle of the road, wanting to melt away, wanting the earth to open up; Sam so pale, so drawn, so wan.

"Gee, Mr. Vaughan . . ."

"Don't you ever put my Rose on your bike again. You keep your hands off my girl. You, you—*boy*. I ought to tan your hide, but I'll leave that for your father when you get home. You stay away from my Rose. We're not having hanky-pankies in this street. We're stopping it, right here and now."

Everyone must have heard. You could hear the windows—and the doors. But that's the way he had always been. Great big loud-mouthed man.

"Never seen her in such a state before. She's only *ten*. I'm surprised you've got the nerve to come home in daylight, bold as brass. All the cheek in the world."

Dad was coming, looking gray.

"I'm sorry, Mr. Vaughan. I didn't mean any harm."

"Sam!" That was Dad's call. "Come on home."

But Vaughan had gone, stamping up his path, up the steps and inside. In behind his door that slammed.

"Come on, Sam."

Following Dad. Oh gawd, following him home.

"Dad."

"Yes."

"Has Rose come home?"

"Didn't you expect her to?"

"I've been looking for her all afternoon."

"What did you do to her?"

"Nothing."

"*What did you do to her?*"

"*Nothing!*"

"I don't believe you."

"Gee, Dad."

"Go to your bed. I'll deal with you there."

But it was Mum who came, Mum who sat on the bed. He felt her weight bear down, but he wouldn't look up at her, and kept his face to the wall.

"What happened, Sam?"

"Nothing."

"There's been an awful row."

"I didn't do anything. If Rose says I did, it's a lie."

"I don't think Rose has been telling tales, I don't think so; it's not come from her at all, but she was in a dreadful state when she came home. I'm dismayed, Sam, not only by what you've done, but by your insistence that you've done nothing."

"I didn't. I didn't."

After a while Dad came and hit him very hard eight times.

Seven

STANDING in the rain.

Her hair in the wind blooming up. Those eyes of hers in the shadow, in the cone of the umbrella; they're a mystery story, Sam.

Oh, she's so beautiful. Like the sun coming up shining through rain. But can't you do more than nod, Sam? Can't you make a noise? Are you to be struck dumb for the rest of your life, boy?

"Well, what have you been yelling for? I hope it's not a joke. You look all right to me. Tricking people on wet days like this isn't very funny."

His nodding changed to a vigorous shaking, a denial, but already he was feeling silly. You'd have to be silly, to be standing in teeming rain like that as if you didn't have the sense to get out of it. "Sam," he said to himself, "she'll be thinking you're soft in the head."

"What's all the mud about?" she asked. "Have you been digging yourself a hole? Did you fall in it?"

Oh, that was cruel, and out it came at last, his hoarse and hurt voice, with the story of his life in breathless sentences. "I was stuck under the church. That's where I was. Stuck there. All night I've been there. I've been trying to get out for ages. Stuck there. It was awful. I thought I was going to die there."

Long before he was through, her grimace told him of her impatience with all his tumbling words, and that made it worse, because he couldn't stop until he had had his say.

"Well, you didn't die," she said. "Did you?"

He nodded again, prickling from discomfort, too humiliated to try again with words.

"You'd better come under my umbrella then, unless you really like standing out in the rain. But don't you get your mud on me. How long have you had those clothes on? A week? A month? Are you bleeding? Is that blood?"

He ran his hand down his bare leg.

"Have you been in a fight?"

Coping with her questions bewildered him, but *that* question was stupid. "I've been stuck under the church," he said indignantly. "Who'd I be fighting under there?"

"I'm sure I don't know. You look as if you've been fighting everybody. Is it one night you've been under there or have you been living there for weeks? What's your mother going to say? Or does she live under there too?"

He stood beside her, awkwardly under the umbrella, lost in embarrassment.

"How long have you been yelling?"

"Oh, a long time."

"Were you yelling at about half-past seven?"

"I don't know." The injustice of her manner suddenly provoked him; suddenly he flared at her with spirit. "I don't even know what time it is now. Didn't I tell you I'd lost me gold watch? If you heard me, why didn't you come?"

"I did come," she said sharply. "I came at half-past seven and at half-past eight and I'm here again. That's three times. What more do you want?"

"You could have told me you were here. You could have called out or something. Then I'd have known."

"Well, I didn't. I'm not a great big man with bulging muscles to look after myself. I didn't know what was going on. Blue murder or what. What *was* going on? What were you stuck under the church for?"

Sam couldn't cope. Oh, it was such a disappointment, and she was so pretty. He wanted so much to impress her. His face twisted up and he sighed. "I do it for fun. It's me hobby. I'm always getting stuck under churches."

"That's childish," she said. "Have you run away because you can't live at home any more? Have you left home because you're sixteen?"

Sam felt himself nodding again; felt that to be sixteen might be the answer.

"Are you sure you're sixteen?"

Sam went on nodding, feeling more and more like sixteen with every nod.

"You don't look sixteen to me."

"I am."

"In short pants?"

His eyebrows came darkly together. "I'm sixteen. I ought to know. . . . And I haven't got any long pants. . . . Like maybe you haven't got a proper overcoat." He was sorry for that; straightaway sorry. He didn't want to be nasty, but she was walking all over him, making such a fool of him.

"I didn't mean that," he said.

She glanced at him, as if she hadn't cared much anyway—almost a glance of scorn. Her eyes seemed to be mocking him all the time, even when her attention appeared to be somewhere else. Moment by moment he felt more and more inadequate, less and less a match for her. Was she playing some kind of game? Was it a grown-up game that he had not yet learned to recognize or understand?

"You're really bleeding, aren't you?" she said. "What *were* you doing under that church? All those scratches and bruises. All that mess. Have you had your breakfast yet?"

He sighed almost tiredly. "Where would I be getting breakfast under there?"

"I'll fix something for you. You can come to my house if you like."

He shook his head emphatically. "I can't—"

"Why not?"

"I can't. What about your mother? What about the people in your house?"

Her lips compressed in irritation. "Are you frightened of people? Have you done something you shouldn't have? Murdered somebody or something? Was that what I was hearing? Have you run away from an orphanage? Have you escaped from prison?"

"Of course I haven't."

She went briefly silent and might have looked puzzled,
or perhaps he imagined that along with everything else.
"There's no one at home, anyway," she said. "Dan's gone out
with his cart. I couldn't come over here again until he'd gone.
Will you come back with me if no one's home?"

"I suppose so—"

"We've got eggs. I'll give you boiled eggs and toast. You'll
behave properly?"

She was so near to him that it was taking his breath away,
but she couldn't have known, could she? No one would do
that deliberately. Or was it all part of the game? Then he was
left stranded in the rain, left disconcerted, and at a loss what
to do. She glanced back impatiently, as if to call him, and
he went after her clumsily, out through the gateway, too
shy to move in with her under the umbrella, too shy even
to walk beside her perhaps a pace removed because he saw
that she carried herself like a woman and he felt much too
young to be close to her. She'd be all of seventeen, easily seventeen, maybe more. He had not seriously noted that before.
Perhaps she'd start running now because of the rain, but no,
she strolled.

It was a graveled road that seemed to be separate from the
rest of the world and he had no memory of it, couldn't
remember it from the night. He must have come such a long
way in the dark. Must have walked so much farther than he
supposed. There was the church behind him and her house
a couple of hundred yards farther on, all but hidden by wil-
low trees or peppercorn trees or something of the sort, but
nothing else distinctive at all. Gum trees, of course, practically everywhere, and pines, and rain and puddles and
mud.

"Come along," she said. She was having trouble with the

umbrella in the wind. Another reason for keeping away—
she might have poked out his eyes.

"I'm coming," he said, but continued to keep his distance,
limp and drenched with rain.

"You're the oddest boy I ever knew, I think. What's wrong
with you?"

"Nothing."

"What's your name?"

He swallowed in alarm. Oh, what was his name? But he
heard himself saying, "Sam." Oh, he should have said Tom
or Dick or Harry—anything but Sam.

"Where do you live, Sam?"

He didn't know. He had not had time to think up the an-
swers. "Nowhere."

"Don't be stupid," she said crossly, and glared back impatiently, as if he were a small child.

"I'm on my way," he stammered, "on my way to my
auntie's. That's what I mean."

"Where does your auntie live?"

"Up the Murray. Yeh, up in New South Wales. That's
where I'm going—New South Wales."

"You haven't got far so far, have you?"

"Depends where I started from!" But his defiance sounded
hollow, and his thoughts were scattered because she was
bullying him. He wished she'd leave him alone; he was tired
of questions.

"How are you getting to New South Wales?"

Sullenly, he said, "It's not any business of yours."

"Isn't it really? It's my business to come out in the pouring rain for you, isn't it? It's my business to give you breakfast, isn't it?"

A sigh rose up from inside. "I'm going by train—if you've
got to know. I've got the fare in my pocket."

"Show me."

"Gee," he cried. She had no right to run him into a corner. "I don't have to show you anything."

"You're lying, Sam, if Sam's your name. You haven't got the fare at all, have you? Where would a boy like you get money like that?"

"I have got the fare and it is my name. I've got two and sixpence."

"You? With two and sixpence? Of honest money? Show me?"

"No."

But his fingers went creeping for it, down beside his trousers pocket, and loudly he jingled the coins so she could hear. Perhaps he'd expected a louder noise, but he said, "Do you believe me now?"

"I'll *bet* it's not two and sixpence."

She stalked ahead then, or perhaps wind caught the umbrella and tossed her on through her front gate, which she appeared to flick shut with a quick movement of her wrist— or was that, too, a trick of the wind? The wooden gate slammed into him, as if specifically to wound him, and if he had not been quick enough it would have pinned his right foot by a picket to the ground.

He leaned against the gate, almost physically sick, almost at the point of swearing at her and running the other way— but he was wet and cold and hungry and so terribly tired. He lifted the catch and meekly followed her to the shelter of the veranda. There she was shaking the umbrella and kicking off her rubber boots.

"Get those things off," she said. "You can't come inside like that."

"Get what off?"

"Those filthy boots. That disgusting overcoat. You know

what I mean. Do you go into your own house like that?"

He sighed. "No, I don't."

"Leave the boots there," she said, "and hang the coat on the nail—and don't touch a thing until you're thoroughly scrubbed."

She sounded like somebody's mother, instead of about seventeen.

Inside was a narrow and gloomy passage, and a strange smell, not unpleasant, but unrecognizable. "In there," she said. "That's the bathroom. I'll bring you some hot water for the bath."

The bathroom looked like a walled-up porch that someone had blocked off as an afterthought. He drooped into its semi-darkness, its only window a small opaque highlight practically out of reach. There was a bath of very old galvanized iron, and a small gray table bearing a small gray dish beneath a small gray mirror. Everything looked so gray—even the walls and the towels and the soap.

Was it the day?

Sam sat miserably on the edge of the bath before remembering the instruction not to *touch*. He sighed again, but couldn't care any more. He couldn't float fifty feet above the ground, could he?

The girl appeared with a large black kettle.

"Stand aside," she said, "or you'll be getting scalded. For heaven's sake, couldn't you have switched on the light? Couldn't you have put the plug in the bath? You'll have to have a stand-up wash, anyway, unless you like sitting in a puddle. There's not enough hot water to make a proper bath. When you get those stinking clothes off, leave them outside the door."

"I—can't—take—my—clothes—off."

"Are you going to have a bath with them on?"

He hung his head, felt so embarrassed, so frightened. Oh, what was he to do? Oh, he should not have come into this house.

"Men," she snorted, "the vanity of them. They're all the same. Sixteen or sixty. I'm *not* going to look at you; I've got better things to do with my time. And for heaven's sake put some cold water in the bath or you'll boil alive. When you're ready, give me a call and I'll bring you a nice hot towel."

Off she went, and the door clicked shut, but there was no proper lock to secure it, not even a bolt to shoot across on the inside.

Oh gawd, the different ways that different people lived. Auntie would have died. She would. She'd have died on the spot without a bolt to shoot across.

And it was much the same for Sam. You get used to bolts; you get used to locks; you get used to being able to shut yourself inside.

The girl had switched on the light—a bare weak globe it was, up against the ceiling—but he would rather have stayed in the dark, secure. I mean, it was all sorts of things, wasn't it; not being scared only of her, but being scared of his own body, of what injuries he might be finding there. Oh, so slowly he got those clothes off, so slowly.

He was blue with bruises from his ribs to his thighs. Gawd, just look at it. Blood still beading on his right hip; blood still beading on his knees. But why didn't it hurt? To look at it you would have thought the pain would have been driving him half mad.

"Where are your clothes?"

"Don't—don't you come in!"

"I can't clean your clothes for you and I can't dry them for you if you don't give them to me, can I? If you don't put them out, I'll have to come in."

"Oh, please. Oh, please don't." He choked up on the fright of it. "Oh, go away, then I'll put them there."

She sounded impatient. "I'm going, I'm going. But be quick about it. And don't spend half an hour in there either. I don't want people coming home and finding you here."

Sam choked up again. "Aren't you allowed—?"

"Allowed what? Allowed to have strange young men in the house? In the bath? What do you think? Are you allowed to have strange girls in your house in the bath?"

Honest. The fright of it was worse than being hit with a stick. His heart must have dropped half a mile at least, down into the earth somewhere.

"You shouldn't have asked me here. Oh, you shouldn't have."

"It's done now. Pass your clothes out. Come on. You can't wear them as they are. You know you can't put them back on until they're clean and dry, so stop being silly."

Getting his breath in an orderly fashion was almost beyond him. Oh, it was awful. "Go away, please," he pleaded.

"I'm gone. I'm gone."

He swept his things into a heap and thrust them through the doorway—opening the door and closing it in a single motion, almost with his eyes shut, trying to cover himself by not looking, but certain she had not gone away at all. Oh, the embarrassment. Oh, the shame.

He leaned trembling against the door, fighting for his breath, striving to become calm, but afraid to leave the door, afraid to go to the bath, although that puddle of water must have been quickly turning cold. What had he done? Oh, what had he done? Now he had nothing to wear. Now he was exposed to view—and to ridicule. No girl had ever seen him without clothes before; never, in his whole life, as far as he knew.

"I can't hear you in the bath," she called. "Your breakfast's cooking. It'll be spoiled."

She sounded like Mum.

"What's wrong with you? Are you sick?"

"No."

"You're being silly, Sam."

He could hardly hear her for the thundering of his pulse, for the beating of it in his head, from the simple embarrassment of being a boy.

Limply, he slid away from the door as if his body had become a structure without bones, so frightened of the situation, and of her, not even knowing her name.

The water was still warm, what there was of it, about an inch in the bath, and shaking with nerves he washed himself in the puddle it made, sitting in it miserably, the water first turning pink with blood and then yellow with mud, and he had to finish off under the tap that gushed with cold, that stung fiercely, and almost cauterized him with its chill. It left him shaking violently, uncontrollably, perhaps from the shock of it, but probably because he was in the same house with her.

"I'm ready for the towel," he cried, hunching low in the bath, his teeth chattering, his voice unrecognizable, the words sounding like anything but what they were.

The door at once opened narrowly, a towel dropped to the floor, and the door closed.

Eight

SAM SHUFFLED to the end of the passage to where he guessed
the kitchen had to be, with the wet towel wound at his waist
and tightly tucked in, so weak and defenseless and confused
that it was only with difficulty he could stand on his feet.
Already the towel was soiled; already there were smears
where it brushed his knees, blood smears and mud smears
that the bath had not fully removed. She'd be cross with him
again. She'd ridicule him again. Oh, *why* had she been there to
block his run from the church out into the world? By now
he could have been miles away instead of here, holding to a
doorjamb with a knuckled white hand, confronted by un-
reachable clothing he couldn't wear drying on chair backs
about the wood stove, and sickened by the smell of cooking
fat in the pan, by smoke and steam and the nerve-racking
presence of her, sickened and frightened of everything he
could think of and see.

She held a knife or an egg lifter or something of the kind
and her soft hair parted from her face disconcertingly, just
like veils, the look of her grabbing at him inside. He couldn't
handle the moods, couldn't handle his terror of her and the
fascination of her at the same time. She looked so slight now,
so small, so different from before. There seemed to be so
little of her that possibly she was only a young girl after all.
How could he have been scared? Perhaps not seventeen, perhaps not that. Oh, she could have been anything—fourteen or
sixteen or grown-up by years—and closely, like a military
inspection, her eyes were traveling the length of him from

his bare feet to the top of his head, to his half-dried hair lank and wild, and down again, as if she saw his injuries, but didn't care, as if he were a picture in a frame she could put up or take down and in the end ignore. So his fright returned.

"Sit there," she said.

It was a scrubbed pine table like Mum's at home, with a small square of linen set for him, with toast waiting and milky tea recently poured in a large china mug. It was so hot and so close and so gloomy in the kitchen that the flames made molten lights on the walls, yet he shivered with nerves and would have loved a blanket across his shoulders to protect him from the world. This she apparently failed to observe.

"Help yourself," she said. "It's all there. It's all yours. Fried eggs coming, not boiled. I thought you'd like them better fried. With fried bread."

He scarcely heard.

"Go on," she said, without looking his way. "Get started, Sam. If anybody ever needed a feed it's got to be you."

But somehow he couldn't start; the will wasn't there. He sat shivering, back slumped, arms limply crossed in his lap, ready to cry, trying not to fall apart, trying to be a "proper" boy who could endure humiliation and bear a pain like the heroes of the history books who had steel in their veins, but his shoulders were shaking and he had to force his eyes shut to imprison the tears. But he could not imprison them; out they came around the edges and there was nowhere for Sam to go. Nowhere to go.

Oh please. I mustn't cry, mustn't cry. I mustn't cry with her here. Not in front of her.

But there was nowhere to go.

Something came down, warm and firm against his head,

against his hair, as warm as the blanket he had hoped for, but it was alive, oh most beautifully alive. An arm took his shoulders and turned him strongly in his chair and drew him forward in against her breast, safe and secure, into the most beautiful refuge he had ever found, drew him in as even his mother had never done.

There's a time, Sam, when mothers leave off and others begin.

She held him there, held his face close to her, cradling him, and with exquisite gentleness stroked his skin with her finger tips and whispered for him to hear, "You've been hurt. Who hurt you, Sam? Who bruised you, Sam? Not under the church. It didn't happen there. Let me make you better, Sam. Let me take away the pain."

He felt her lips kiss his hair.

"There, there. It's all right, Sam. I'm not going to sneer."

He clung to her as he had never clung to anyone, as if after a long journey of fourteen years and four months and nine days, he had come home.

Nine

FIRMLY, SHE pulled away from him.

"Sam," she said in a moment, sounding almost stern.

Firmly away, and succeeding at the second try, but not hurting his pride, as if breaking away at this point were the proper thing to do, as if it were part of the universal plan to say that enough was enough, but she'd still be around at another time.

Well, that was how it got through to Sam, as if someone had murmured it in a noisy room—the feeling happening at that threshold where you can never be sure you've got the message right or upside down.

"Sam," she said, "food costs money."

He had not expected her to follow up with *that*—like eggs are a shilling a dozen and the flag is red, white, and blue, or something of the kind. Almost sounded as if she meant it for some other fellow who must have come yesterday and was still in hiding behind the door. So he sat for a while bewildered in his chair, trying to work out whether the whole thing was real or bits from a book he'd read somewhere.

But you couldn't push it off the edge into fantasy land. It had happened, you know, and he had been there. Oh boy, oh wow. No one else was telling him about it—he had been there! He had been the fella! A real live living girl as soft as dreams and as firm as now had been hanging onto him as if she'd been waiting for a year for him to arrive. Oh boy, what a snuggle. She was beautiful, she was lovely, she was better than all the Christmases that ever were. Holding on to her was like leaving the earth behind. It was, you know. Like taking off with the wings of a bird. Hear those wings flapping, boy, up past the rooftops, out round the steeples, way up in the clouds. Oh wow. As if everything solid had melted and there was nowhere hard to fall. Oh, the change. The change in this girl.

"Sam, do eat up your breakfast."

He looked up at her, trying to relate to her extraordinary words, trying to see her through a fog of mysteries, a fog of dreams, through all the flapping wings and the clouds.

Breakfast?

"You're lovely," he said, swaying his head like a wise old owl, knowing it had to be the right thing to say, though no one had told him, that he could recall, no one in the whole wide world, and she smiled.

The longer he looked at her the more like perfection she became, as if she had been growing lovelier every day for a couple of million years.

Yeh. No kidding.

"How old are you, hey?"

And fancy asking her, straight out, as if he wasn't even scared!

But she shook her head. "Old enough, Sam."

"If you're going to be my girl I've got to know. Not knowing isn't fair."

"Perfectly fair. Ladies don't say how old they are."

"Gee, you've changed."

"From what?"

But how could he answer her? How could he tell her she had been so awful before? He went embarrassed again and felt naked again, though being wrapped up in that towel, when you really got down to thinking about it, was like wearing about half a mile of fabric straight off the roll.

"Come on, come on, Sam. Your tea and toast will be cold and we can't throw food away. And your eggs will spoil if I don't get them out of the pan."

"What's your name?"

"Rose."

He watched her move to the stove. She was nothing like Rose. That was silly—calling her Rose, like calling somebody else Sam, when it was *his* name. Rose was thirteen now and still shrank into something tiny when you tried to hold her hand. Rose liked to be near him and was never far from his

side when it was safe to be so, but say anything the slightest
bit soppy to Rose and she ran away.

"You've changed," he said, getting the tone into his voice
that seemed to say, "I don't understand."

"No, Sam. Just the same. . . . Your eggs. Fried hard. . . .
Oh, Sam, like leather! Well, that's how you'll have to eat
them. Come on, I've never seen such a dream."

She sat away from him, sideways on a chair; sidesaddle,
you could say (the way Rose sat on the bicycle bar), but
with one bare foot hooked by the heel over a rail. Oh, just
as graceful as Rose. Maybe *this* Rose *was* a ballet star. There
was nothing as lovely as her, there wasn't, not anywhere he
had ever been, nothing as graceful or as poised, with a face
so fragile an artist might have painted her hundreds of years
ago on the ceiling of a chapel among the angels in the clouds.
Her clothing had no shape at all, or color either that he could
later say. Maybe it was brown or gray, but it only made
her lovelier somehow, lovelier and lovelier every moment
he held her with his eyes.

Oh, Sam, is she really your girl? Does it happen this way?
Suddenly you've got a girl and nothing else matters any
more? Maybe you can still go home and straighten things
out with Lynch and with Mum. Yeh. Then you can come
back to see her every day. Tuning in to girls: oh, such a sudden thing. A girl jumps up like a spring and nothing else
matters any more. Heartbeat thundering now, but nothing
like the thunder of before, nothing like the thunder of fear
that had shaken him behind the bathroom door. It was strange.
The change. The way things take a turn.

He hoped she might come over again and hold him by the
shoulders again and press his face against her again—how
could she help herself if the feelings inside her were any-

thing like his own? But there she sat on the edge of her chair
sipping tea through a veil of hair. She didn't come, but didn't
run away either. She was still there.

Oh, Sam. . . .

His eyes dropped to the breakfast she had prepared and
hunger became an awareness again, became sharp again, and
when he looked up with a mouthful of something or other,
she smiled. If the eggs were like leather, he didn't notice. If
food had gone cold, he didn't care. His hunger became a
ravenous compulsion to clear the table of whatever was there,
to recharge with energy indiscriminately, and to be done with
it all. Would she kiss him then? Could he hold her shoulders
and kiss her hair? Still sitting there, she was, white cup in
hand, a beautiful slender hand, and a glint of gold.

Something about the gold he had not got on to before—
the shape of it and where she wore it.

On her wedding finger she had a ring of gold.

He stared in unbelief, a pain catching at him inside, actually taking away his breath.

Over and over he said it, *she's married, she's married*, over
and over, but there wasn't any sound.

Palaces fell down. Castles vanished from the air. It was as
if the spark that had made him into Sam had gone and left
behind a body that didn't care whether it remained a person
or became a piece of stone.

She was watching him with eyes different from before,
with troubled eyes, with shadows there.

"Sam," she said.

"You're married. . . ."

Her foot slipped from the chair rail to the floor and she
looked odd, and disturbed, and said sharply, almost angrily,
"I didn't say I wasn't. Does it matter if I'm married?"

"You're married. . . ."

"How can it affect you whether I'm married or not?"

Inside him there was more pain than he knew how to bear. "You kissed my hair—"

She shook her head, showing the white of teeth. "Sam—what on earth has being married got to do with kissing your hair?"

He hung his head.

In an agitated way, she started shaking out his clothing, knocking off crisp mud, changing things around in front of the stove to speed the drying.

"You're not being fair, Sam. You shouldn't make a thing of it. It was to make you better. It was to show someone cared."

"But you're married."

"I didn't hide my hand." She sounded breathless now. "It was on view all the time. You must have seen the ring there. I didn't hide it from you, Sam. Now look, you don't fall in love in five minutes. You don't fall in love with everyone you meet. You don't fall in love with people you don't even know. You're only a boy. I kissed your hair. All right. To comfort you, as any woman worth her salt would have done, I'm sure."

He sobbed, but not with tears that she could see or hear. "You had it all worked out, didn't you, to make a fool of me."

"That's not true, Sam."

"I think it is. All that kissing and being kind. All those soppy words. It was a game for you."

"It wasn't a game then, Sam, and it still isn't. It seems to me you didn't understand. Just two people being nice to each other. Two people hanging on to each other for a little bit of comfort. I've not done anything wrong, nor have you. We've done nothing but show each other a bit of tenderness. If you can't do that, why bother to be alive at all?"

"I thought you were my girl."

She turned away with the suddenness of exasperation, and seemed to be looking outside into a wet, gray yard where thousands of empty bottles were stacked about six feet high.

"I'm much older than you, Sam; you must know that. I never took it for a moment that you didn't know. But you're a nice boy. You're a good-looking boy. It was nice to comfort you. It was nice for me and it was nice for you. I couldn't be the first young woman to say nice things to you. . . ."

Her eyes came round.

"Oh, Sam, am I?"

There was nothing for him to say. Everything felt like the end of the world.

She came back to him, came close to him, but he flinched and shrank, just like Rose on the hillside when she was ten years old.

"Sam, don't spoil something that's nice. Don't turn it into an ugliness, Sam. You said you were sixteen—are you fifteen—oh—are you fourteen? Sam—only fourteen. . . ."

Gently she touched his hair.

"Go away."

"You were hurt, Sam. You had a fight, and I was on your side. All those cuts and hurts. It does things to a woman to see a boy hurt. I wanted to comfort you. Surely you understand?"

But he didn't understand.

"You must allow me to help you—to dress your wounds—"

"I want my clothes. I want to go."

She looked like a woman now. Really and truly. She might have been twenty even. He was so ashamed. Twenty—and married. It was like not knowing what day it was or forgetting that twice two is four. Not knowing she was *old*.

She sighed. "Your clothes are all there. Your boots are in the hearth. Oh, Sam. . . ."

She shook her head and walked from the room, her soft hair blooming about her as before, but making him feel dreadful now. The back door slammed and she went barefoot into the yard.

Ten

SAM WAS half a mile down the road before he felt for his money. Perhaps he had been worrying about the suspicion that it wasn't feeling heavy enough where the weight of it bore against his thigh. It was doing a lot of jingling, but maybe should have jingled more.

Heaven knows where, in reality, he was heading by then, and it didn't matter much. He had blundered out of the house, blundered onto the street, blundered off, clothes still half wet, still struggling hundreds of yards from the gates with buttons that wouldn't push into holes, half-swearing, half-weeping, and feeling such a fool, which was worse. As if he must have been so green it was a wonder people weren't mistaking him for a paddock of grass.

The railway had to be *that* way, north, a couple of miles, and he was trying to head in its direction, but was frustrated

because there weren't any roads across and he was too nervous to trust the foot tracks or animal tracks or whatever
they were. This was all orchard, with rough-looking patches
of scrub in between, strung out in a straight line into the
east, fruit trees without leaves pruned bare and stark and
no one about to work in the wet. It was cold, with an icy
breath and a blackness in the sky that people might say held
snow, though Sam had never seen snow and wasn't keen to
start breaking with the tradition just yet. That would have
been too much like the orphan thrown out—the way it happened in those old melodramas when you were pretty sure
you were not supposed to bleed about it much, but as soon as
you laughed along with everybody else you started thinking
how terrible it would be in real life.

So he thrust a worried hand into his trousers pocket and
felt around for his loose change and brought it up in fright—
four pennies, two lousy half-pennies, and two threepenny
bits.

No matter how long he'd be staring at it, aghast, it would
never be adding up to two shillings and sixpence—not in this
life, mate, or the next—and a new kind of panic went dropping into that bottomless pit where his stomach used to be.

Not even half left of what he had started out with. Where
could you go for elevenpence? I mean *where*? To the city
and back? Oh, marvelous. In the other direction to the end
of the electric line perhaps? What use was that? He could
walk it in a few hours, in a day at the most, and Lynch or
the police or someone would catch up so easily it was
scarcely worth the effort of running away in the first place.

It was right, you know. Without your bike you're nothing.
You're not a person any more. With a bike in your hands
even losing money is not the end of the world—you can

get in that saddle and push those pedals and go. Without your bike you're stuck; you turn into a snail.

A boy's got to move.

"When you're down, Sam," Dad had a habit of saying, particularly of late, "you're down—and out for the count. Everyone's in for a kick at the corpse. It takes more than a day to get up."

Every pocket, every single pocket he frantically emptied out—mushy bits of paper, bits of string, stub of a pencil, penknife, wet fluff, dirt, but nothing that looked like cash, and already he had turned around, already he was walking back, then he was running with the remnants of his money clenched in his fist, fright and anger and resentment boiling over into a blind rush. But it was too far back—too far for running so strenuously even for the righteous indignation of beating on her door and yelling to high heaven: "You rotten thief. Give me back my money. I didn't want you doing things for me. Did I ask? You've got no right paying yourself out of my pocket for things when I didn't ask." But he couldn't last the distance, not the way he felt.

He collapsed on a stump, a wet tree stump that struck like a puddle through to his skin in seconds, and he went on sitting there waiting for the sickness inside him to sink back into place, to sink back, to lie still.

Farther along the road he could see the house looking like something he didn't want to go to any more. It was an uneasy feeling, as if something that should have gone right had gone wrong. Something had happened there that had not belonged; something good had taken the wrong twist. All those empty bottles stacked in heaps in the yard. That's what her "Dan" must have been—a buyer and seller of bottles. That's where he had gone with his cart. "Bottle-o! Bottle-o!"

And home he'd come each night, clanking like O'Grady's ghost.

Sam didn't like empty bottles; didn't like what they meant, men getting drunk and staggering about—he was frightened of drunks; didn't like the smoke scudding from the chimney in the wind (so desperately wild it looked); didn't like thinking of the plates he had eaten from and the cup he had drunk from, left on the table turning greasy and cold.

He felt so sick. He just couldn't be sick; couldn't afford to be sick; couldn't afford to lose those eggs. They must have been the dearest eggs in the history of the world! Such a shocking waste. But up they came. Up they came, practically tearing him apart.

After that, what was the point?

Some aspects are not favorable. There are times when locations are not right. All the signs are there but they don't snap into place. It's best to get away even if you haven't got a bike. Even if you have to walk. The snail, if he crawls for long enough, crosses the path.

Eleven

THE MAN in the railway ticket box looked like a face behind bars in jail. Maybe he was in for a gentlemanly act of polite embezzlement—didn't look like a proper crook. He had a sandy gray mustache that drooped an inch at the end and glasses without frames. They sat on the bridge of his nose— people called them pince-nez. What was his view of Sam? Much the same—a face behind bars like a face in jail.

Sam said quietly, so quietly that no one on this earth could hear: "How far can I go for eightpence?"

"Speak up," the man with the mustache said. "Pro-*ject* the voice, boy."

"Eightpence," said Sam. "How far can I go?"

"Well, it won't be for an ocean voyage or a luxury cruise, we can be sure of that. Why should you ask?"

"Because I want to know."

Because he wanted to know! That kid out there looking tired and pale and strained wanted to know. Hard day for kids not long out of school wanting to know. Picking them was a ticket-seller's game—if the station master had stepped out for a while or had the flu and had stopped in bed with the sporting page. Well, perhaps not a game, though who can be sure from so many years off? Sitting in a ticket box for a man of that kind cannot make for memorably exciting days.

"Depends," the man said, "which way you want to go, whether you're coming back again and when, and how old you estimate you are. If you're under fourteen, you can go twice as far."

"I'm thirteen."

"If you're thirteen, I'm my own Aunt Regina aged ninety-three."

"Well, I'm not twelve any more."

"With that I might agree," the man said. "I'll not be twelve any more either—thank the Lord—but if you say you're thirteen it's on your head, not mine."

"I had elevenpence," Sam said, "but had to use threepence for a meat pie." He was going to say that he had had two and six, but she had taken it. Then changed his mind. "I was sick, too."

"Because of the pie?" the man asked. "Always regard them with suspicion, boy."

"No, sir."

"You mean you were sick before the pie?"

"Yes, sir."

"And then you ate the pie?"

"Yes, sir."

"I understand," the man said, "why you're looking pale. . . . Well, where do you want to go? To the country or the sea or Timbuktu?"

Sam looked down. "I want to go a long way. A long way. I want to go a long way."

When Sam looked up again, two pale blue eyes were peering into his.

"You've thought this over?"

"Yes, sir."

"Good and hard?" The man tapped his brow. "In here? Up top?"

"Yes, sir."

"At thirteen you're too young to be on your own. There are laws, and rightly so. You should still be in school. The truant inspector will be after you and he's a mean man. And what'll your mother say? But if you're fourteen there's a chance they'll leave you alone."

"If I'm fourteen, I can't go as far."

"That's true. Perhaps you can be thirteen today and fourteen tomorrow?"

"Yes, sir."

"I think you ought to go away from the sea. You might be tempted into the city, boy, and you could end up in some flea-ridden rooming house—or in very bad company—or in jail. The city's a hard place for a boy running away. Everywhere's a hard place for a boy running away. There are nasty people in the world."

"I didn't say I was running away."

"No, you didn't. I'm making a philosophic comment upon what I divine the situation to be. You could go to upper Fern Tree Gully."

"That's not far."

"Nothing that stops at this station goes any farther today. Have you been there?"

"No."

"Well, now's the time. You can change there to the steam train on narrow gauge and that'll go over the top to Gembrook. Gippsland begins out there. I've always liked the sound of Gippsland, boy; always liked the look of the word. What about you?"

"I haven't thought about it, sir."

"Good country if you keep to the roads. Fresh farm food growing everywhere, poking up out of the ground. Lots of milk and cream. How does that appeal to you?"

"Sounds all right, sir."

"But you've got the mountains first and they'll be cold this time of year. Maybe snow. Snowing up there today, they tell me. Very cold out of doors. Cold enough here. Keep under cover. Understand? Don't go sleeping in the open or wriggling into culverts or up hollow logs. None of that nonsense. Too much going on you can't see. Find a place to sleep, boy, while there's daylight to look around."

"I've got an auntie."

"They've all got aunties. Where's yours?"

"Up the Murray, sir. Up in New South Wales. It's not cold up there."

"Don't you believe it. Inland, on the plains? This time of

year? Skies like crystal. Frosts like you've never seen. Freeze
your eyebrows off, boy. And you can't go two hundred miles
for eightpence." His voice dropped. "Not even with me.
What's your auntie's name? I'll wager you don't know. The
Murray's not a good idea, boy. Too far. Too much can go
wrong on the way. Miles and miles and miles without people.
Hard country these days. Everything's failed. Everyone's
gone broke. You'll end up dead in a ditch down some deserted
back road, unless you like eating nardoo seed or witchety
grubs or the roots of mulga trees, and I never knew a white
kid yet with the brains to live off the land. Tell you what
we'll do. You keep your eightpence, you hang on to it while
you can, and I'll see you at the bottom end of the platform
when it's time for the next train."

"But my ticket—?"

"Don't be dumb—or I might change my mind. You have
to be sharp to survive. You have to be sharp, boy, or I'll
be hurting you by putting you on that train."

Sam traveled in the guard's van and sat on a crate of chickens
three months old.

"Mo and his lame dogs," the guard grumbled, blowing his
whistle and waving his flag and slamming his door, "why
can't he charge a fare for a change? Stopping here is gettin'
to be a problem. I reckon we should start runnin' express
to Tunstall. Now look here, kid—what's your name?"

"Bob."

"All right, Bob, you listen here. If anyone wants to know,
they're your chooks, see, and you're ridin' with them because
they're a special breed and they get lonely."

"What special breed?" said Sam.

"They're your chooks, aren't they? Why ask me? Any
ticket inspectors get on this train, you get off, see, because

they'll be trouble for both of us. I'll know 'em. I'll see 'em. I'll tell you to scat. Right?"

"Yes, sir."

"Any women get in here, any women with babies in prams, you keep your trap shut, see. You be the dumbest kid in sight. You make noises like a mute or something. Right?"

"Yes, sir."

"If you want a cup of tea pour one out of me thermos, but don't go chuckin' it around. It's not for spilling. It's for drinkin' straight down. Flamin' Mo and his lame dogs traveling free. He'll be gettin' lumbered, you know. He'll be waking up one morning and his job'll be gone."

"I think he's a nice man. I think you are, too."

"The Railway Commissioners, Bob, won't be sharin' that view."

But Sam sat on the crate of chickens (though he could have sat on the bench if he had wanted to) feeling nice and warm and vague inside. Feeling pleased. Not feeling deeply or desperately about anything, just sitting there with a little smile because at last a few things seemed not to be kicking him so hard.

That grown-up Rose, that woman, was a shadow, but the guard over there didn't know about her, did he? No one knew. No one here knew about the newspapers either, all over the road, or about the two and sixpence, or about not going home to Wickham Street. No one knew unless he told them. The guard might have been shooting Sam a few quick and thoughtful glances, but he wouldn't be telling anyone anything because he was breaking the rules himself, just as the man in the ticket box had broken the rules, just as grown-up Rose had broken the rules. No one would be finding out about anything until Sam started saying the words himself. It was hard not doing it though; it really was. He usually was the one who told on himself—never told on anyone else, yet told on himself all the time. But not today.

"How'd you get hurt?" the guard said.

But Sam could hardly hear and slowly shook his heavy head as if he wanted everyone to leave him alone. The ticket inspectors didn't get on the train, and no ladies with babies brought their prams, and no one asked what he was doing there, and the bogie underneath the guard's van clattered and clanged and clacked the miles away. It was nice: things being uncomplicated for a change.

There was a rhythm beyond Sam's closed eyes, a rhythm like a small child's cradle clacking on boards. . . .

Whose baby was it in the cradle? That wooden cradle rocking gently on the wooden floor?

When he peeped in, it looked like Sam.

Yeh.

Handsome little kid; I'll say, I'll say.

"He's beautiful," Sam said. "There never was a kid like him, you know."

"There was you," she said.

"You weren't around when I was a baby," said Sam. "You wouldn't know."

"I know all right. There's nothing I don't know about you, Sam Collins."

"Honey, I can't believe he's ours."

"You'd better," she said, "oh, you'd better."

Her head rested against the blue jacket of his uniform. Her cheek reached his wings. When you're six feet two, most of the world is down there, even most of her. Her hand touched his sleeve.

"Oh, do be careful, Sam, in those rotten airplanes."

He moved against her, but made no sound.

"It's not just me, Sam. You've got him to live for now. Oh, Sam, don't go playing big heroes."

"That's not me, love."

"I think it is. What are we going to do, the two of us, when the ship takes you away? We'll be split down the middle. There'll only be halves of us. Half to go and half to stay. Come back, Sam. Come back, Sam."

The guard said, "Wake up, Bob. Stir your bones. Do you hear?"

Sam heard.

"We'll be there in a minute. Upper Gully. End of the line. And when we stop you head for the lavatory, see. Hide there until everything's quiet and everyone's gone. You understand?"

"Yes, sir."

"And don't dob me in if people start askin' questions. Don't tell anyone you traveled free. And don't split on old Mo— he tries to be a friend to kids like you."

"I wouldn't tell, sir. Cross my heart I wouldn't."

"See you remember. Bob, I'm worried about you."

"I'm all right, sir."

"It's very cold out there. Those clothes you're wearing— you could shoot peas through 'em. It's been snowing up here. You've got to be careful; got to keep under cover; got to keep yourself warm. You're too narrow in the chest, boy. What does your mother say?"

Sam sighed and looked away.

"She doesn't approve? I don't either. Look, Bob, I'll take you back again. I'd rather run that risk than let you out here on your own."

Sam's mouth set in a line. "I don't want to go back there."

"I'm givin' you fair warning. If I hear of a kid missin', if you fit the description, I'll have to tell them. And it'll not be for anything I'm likely to gain. It won't do me no good, son, but it'll be in your best interests. I won't be saying you traveled free in the guard's van, but I'll say I saw you here getting off the train."

"That's not fair."

"Oh yes it is. As fair as any honest man can make it. Take this tuppence. It'll buy you a ticket and get you started on the Gembrook line. When you get off then is up to you. Goes so slow uphill you can lean out and pick the daisies anyway. Don't go getting off on bridges though. Don't go getting off in the bush. Don't go acting rash."

"I'm all right."

"Here's a couple of sandwiches I couldn't eat. Stick 'em up your shirt and eat 'em later in the waiting room. Sit there until your train comes in. And no bright ideas in this kind of weather of thumbing a ride out on the road. Buy your tuppenny ticket and you've got as much right as anyone to sit in the waiting room. There'll be a nice fire goin'—or ask the porter to light you one."

The train had stopped and outside it was shockingly cold.

Twelve

EVERYTHING was quiet now except for wind. Everyone had gone now, even the train, blowing its whistle, back to Melbourne, back to Wickham Street, away from the black mountains. Never a blacker day had Sam seen. It was so cold; so wet cold. Was it the coldest day that had ever been?

No Gembrook train came down from the fissure in the mountains, puffing smoke and hissing steam. Milk cans stood abandoned on the platform, and sad chickens drooped in crates out of the rain. Oh, the mountains were so black; so looming black, so brooding black. Forest somehow blacker than night disappeared in sky pressing down and lights across the road in houses shone like yellow holes, though it was only two in the afternoon.

Sam wished he had gone to the sea.

Mountains were not for Sam. How could they have been? He didn't belong. Sore Thumb Sam. He didn't like the lone swift flags of tattered gray swirling up there, clouds against clouds, like separate things alive; didn't like the tall trees quivering as if angry giants shook them at the ground.

The door to the waiting room was closed.

He opened it by the knob and peered inside. Bright firelight flickered on dull green walls. He opened it wider and a young woman with a baby at her tight white breast looked directly into his eyes.

Oh, she was beautiful, like a portrait by an Old Master sitting there. He didn't mean to stare, but her flesh was like milk, something he had never seen before, as if her whole body were of milk for her babe.

"Do you mind?" she said. "It's the Ladies' Room. Can't you read?"

"I'm sorry," Sam said. "Oh, I'm sorry," and quickly shut himself outside.

He stood flaming, grimacing, burning up with blushing, but it didn't say *Ladies' Room*, it didn't say it at all. *Waiting Room* were the words up there on the sign over the door, and below, across the line, beyond the railway yard, was the open road. To where? Why should he look there?

A woman feeding a baby; and so graceful, so beautiful,

though not much more than a grown-up girl, like grown-up Rose. What do you know! Did grown-up Rose have a baby somewhere, in a back room, not seen?

Gee.

What if she came out? What would he do if she came out of there? Where would he look then? Where would he go? What would he say to her?

"Oh, I'm sorry, ma'am; I'm sorry, ma'am. I wasn't really staring. I didn't really see." But he did. Did he ever.

There was the railway timetable, stuck to a notice-board. He peered at it intently, working out the figures, trying to read the language of the rows. The next train for Gembrook didn't leave for ages—and ages, and ages—and there was nowhere to hide away. He couldn't stop in the lavatory for one and a half hours. He'd freeze. And he had stood as much of that place as he could stand before. Didn't they ever clean the place? Maybe it was too much for the porters, too. And he couldn't hang about in the open, doing nothing, getting nowhere. Even if he had not seen the woman with the baby, how could he have sat around for one and a half hours? Like a lifetime, you know? A boy's got to move. A boy's got to go.

Sam walked through the barrier gate, down the long ramp, under the line, and came out at road level into the wet black cold. Water streamed from the embankment making glassy sounds. Mud everywhere; churned-up tracks of horse drays and motor trucks gone away. Air like ice. It was like being where life didn't happen now, where tomorrow wouldn't come, where people came to die. Maybe animals gathered silently in glades and melted.

Oh, the feeling of it; as if desolation was waiting to swallow you whole. White snowflakes in the rain. And there should have been tombstones. Here lies Faith. Here lies Hope. Here lies Charity. Here lies Silly Stupid Sam.

What do you do? Do you give in? Do you go back home? Do you chuck it all and say to the world: "You win. You're too big. You don't play fair."

He could feel snow on his nose and oddly on his fingers when he ran them through his hair, though there was nothing to see except a breath that disappeared. That was snow; real snow falling there, or had he walked into a picture hanging on a wall?

You've got two cheese sandwiches and tenpence in your pocket, Sam, and enough leather on your boots to last for fifty miles. A bit of snow's not going to hurt you, boy. Look at the Eskimos. They serve it up for dinner with fried seal and mixed herbs.

Snow, Sam. Real snow.

Nervously, as if it had to be a dream, he held out a hand, and stared.

There it is in the air. The real thing. Same as on Everest and at the South Pole. Where does it go when it hits the ground? Instantly it's not there.

It's getting thicker and thicker and *thicker* in the air. Hey, get an eyeful, Sam. Would you believe! As light as feathers, as soft as wool, as thick as walls, and you can run through it, Sam. Like flying high, high in the air. Like flying.

Hey, it's like being a bird, snow swirling round you like clouds. Hey, could I fly if I try?

Look, everybody. Snow everywhere. Look at me, Sam, in the snow. I've never seen snow in fourteen years and four months and nine days before. Never, never, never. Gee, would you believe! Snow here. I thought you'd have to go— I don't know—I thought you'd have to go a million miles.

Hey, mister; real snow. I've never seen snow before.

Hey, look, on the ground.

Everywhere. Everywhere lying white on the ground. Everywhere flying in the air, like millions of flowers, like millions of petals, like millions of moth wings, but softer, you know? It's so soft in the air.

Why don't they tell you these things? Why don't they teach you at school? Why don't they say, "Look, kid, go out and find these things, you're alive."

It's so beautiful. It's so clean. Hey, the way it feels in your hands.

"*Hey, mister. Real snow.*"

"Yes, boy, real snow."

"Don't you reckon it's just beautiful, mister?"

"Seeing you enjoy it, boy—yes, I'd say so. Yes, beautiful. But keep off the road. They mightn't all have stopped like me. Some idiot who ought to know better might be driving home."

Oh, swinging under a young and lanky tree, hooked to the trunk by an arm, swinging back and forth on heels and toes, watching the snow come down, watching it eddy (like shuffling cards), watching it roll (like the sea), Sam smiling and biting at his lips and blinking at an emotion that felt like tears.

Oh, gee.

"Does it snow a lot, mister?" Having to shout now because of a muffled feeling, because sounds were locked up in rooms, because the man in the motor truck mightn't hear and it was important that he should. Things have got to be shared.

"About once in seven years."

Hey, God up there. Fancy making something like this out of that awful-looking sky that's disappeared.

You're a genius, I reckon.

Fancy making it once in seven years.

Fancy making it on the day I'm here.

Fancy making it, anyway, and letting it fall.

"You'd better get up beside me, boy," the man said. "You shouldn't be out in it too long."

Sam, that was an invitation to sit up there.

Hey, did you hear it right?

Was it a Ford? Was it a Chev? Was it made of wood? Was it cut out of planks with a canvas hood? It shook as if shivering, as if the cold was getting into its creaking joints. Snow on the front was all heaped up.

"Where are you going, mister?"

"Macclesfield Road, Monbulk."

Sam slowly shook his head. "Where's that, mister? Is it Gippsland? Is it Gembrook? Oh, the snow. Oh, the snow's stopped coming down."

"Boy!"

The voice had become stern. He was a wizened man— and looked like years or very long journeys or crags.

"Yes, sir," said Sam.

The half-door on the passenger side swung open. It was a long stretch up from the ground.

"Come on."

Was it an Austin? Was it a Buick?

Sam threw up a long leg and climbed. Oh, my goodness, up he climbed and sat on a folded burlap bag beside the man. There was snow inside, too. The day of wonders this had to be. Well, he'd sat in the buses on Canterbury Road but that wasn't the same.

Gee.

"Shut the door."

Sam gave it a healthy slam.

Was it a Renault? Was it an Essex?

"No," the man said, "it's not in Gippsland; it's not Gembrook either; but it's in the general direction."

"Oh, the snow. Oh, the snow's all going. Look, it's melting, mister. Doesn't it stay?"

"It might. It might. The day's not over yet by a long shot."

Sam was sitting in a car up front. That was the windshield, close enough to touch. Well, not a passenger car, but a motorcar nevertheless, with cabbage leaves on the tray at the back. There was the steering wheel. There were the clocks. There were the levers the driver had to push.

It was marvelous.

"Boy," the man said, "let's get it straight. Are you a gentleman of the road?"

Something inside Sam clicked. Did he look as desperate as that? His answer became a high-pitched squeak. "You mean a highwayman?"

"Do I mean—no I don't! I mean are you on the road? Are you a tramp? Are you a swaggie?"

Sam thought about it. "Yes," he said. "I'm a swaggie."

"Where's your swag?"

Sam looked across and immediately down in confusion to where a lever shook between the open boards. That's how things happened. The things a fellow never thought of. Grownups were quicker than light. The second you dropped your guard, they had you impaled.

"Where are your blankets, boy? Where's your billycan? Where's your hat? You ought to have a hat. Where's your tea and flour and frying pan?"

Sam grimaced and felt betrayed.

"How long have you been a swaggie, boy?"

"Since yesterday, sir," he sighed.

"My God. Couldn't you have waited until the weather turned warm?"

Sam looked away. He was dead right, of course. What a time to start!

"My name's Hopgood," the man said. "What's yours?"

"Sam."

"Yes, you look like a Sam. But today's not the day for proving any more you're a man. We'll take you home."

There was an explosion inside Sam—oh, such an exploding indignation. "You'll not! You'll not do that to me. I'm fourteen! I only came up here to get out of the snow."

A wiry hand gripped Sam and held him back from the door. It was incredibly strong, that hand; a twist of the fingers or a jerk of the wrist and Sam feared it might have snapped his arm.

"Not your home, Sam. Mine."

The grip relaxed, and Sam unwound as if knots were coming undone painfully inside. For a while in slight bewilderment he slowly rubbed his arm from the hurt, then he looked across at Mr. Hopgood and smiled. He really was an odd little man. How old could he be? Two hundred years? Or did he live in the open where the sun and the rain beat down?

"I've not sat up front next to the driver before," said Sam.

Thirteen

THAT DAY was always separate, always in a black and white box—a day within a day, I guess. They were Sam's memories

—black and white and gray—but not dreary in the least. Startling would be more the word, like opening up the bedroom curtains on a breathtakingly original event. Like looking out at 6 A.M. with sleep in your eyes and a crick in your neck and discovering your house afloat in the midst of icebergs. Just as marvelous; just as marvelous as that.

Oh, the road wound about so much, and swept up and swept down so much, and trees were so stark and deep and tall. So many of them, so many trees, and oh so tall, with trunks like a thousand swaying masts on a thousand swaying ships. Like a vast harbor crowded with ships—ships from every port you could think up. From Freetown and Rio de Janeiro and Vladivostok. Oh, from places you couldn't even spell. It was like that. *Stunning*. To look up on the curves, to lean out and peer up, was to lose your grip on the solid world as if a sea really did sag underneath, and above you all heaven gaped beyond the mast.

Nothing much happened, nothing much, but Sam's senses practically swam. To be sitting up front, up front beside the driver; to see the snow, the mountaintops, the valleys, the villages, to be *moving* like that. To be going somewhere, into places you'd never imagined. To be going downhill and up at forty miles an hour and not having to push—nothing like it had happened to Sam in all his years of life.

Nothing like it ever. These things happen only once and cannot happen twice. You arrive at these points and they are there and everything that happened before is canceled in effect or displaced. It's the king-hit. It becomes the winding-up of aircraft engine revolutions like a siren gaining momentum, like a siren of dire warning running wild, saying it is now, now is the day, now is the time, the time is now.

It becomes the wailing scream of propeller pitch overrunning safe limits and the incredible pressure of flying controls as if no man alive could ever bear the weight, as if no man ever would, and a vibration overwhelms all life as if the gases of the atmosphere are turning into rocks and are battering you to death because the time is now.

Voices from a long way off were shouting inside Sam's head. Oh yes, Sam was there.

"What's wrong with Sam? My God, drag him off."

"Do something there."

"Shift him, will you! Someone shift him. Someone get him off those controls."

Sam could feel hands upon him as if trying to tear his body apart. "Oh leave me be," he cried. "Let me die where I lie." But they couldn't hear because no sound came out.

"Sam's shot. There's blood everywhere."

"For God's sake, we'll never pull out of the dive. That's two hundred and forty knots."

"Malcolm, for God's sake pull us out."

Forty miles an hour, you know? Imagine traveling at a speed like that. Not in a train or anything shared by everyone else—but in a real motor on a winding mountain road sitting up beside the driver. Just you and the driver and no one else. All that power and speed and noise and rattling and shaking—the thrill of it—all happening right there, right here, under your very own feet, until Mr. Hopgood suddenly exclaims, "Great Scott. I'll be killing myself." And dramatically slows up.

Five trees were down, along the miles, though it might have been six, split like sticks from the weight of snow.

"Out you get," Mr. Hopgood said, and out they got, the

two of them, Sam leaping to the road with laughter, with excitement, and dragging knife-sharp branches to the edges and spilling them over, getting the whipback, getting the spray of leaves and twigs and wet. It wasn't living dangerously, but it was living. And down over the edges or up on the high slopes, more trees broke with cannon-shot sounds and snow fell cascading as if waterfalls were let loose.

Sam screamed, "Just look at that."

Oh, a glorious sight, an exhilaration, everything moving with labored grace, boughs and branches and foliage heavy and slow like overloaded boats on heaving oceans. Oh, it was like a projection of storm and motion and delicious peril out near the edges of the planet, out near Cape Horn perhaps, where life could have been real or imagined or dreamed and no one cared which as long as you were there to be in it. Oh, such as assault upon your feelings, such a stunning bewilderment, such a wonderland of cause and effect. And look at that! Gray shreds of mist below and above sweeping by like spirit fragments, like ghosts on secret missions, passing into treetops and vanishing—or coming out in different shapes somewhere else. Stunning. Oh, stunning. Everywhere black and white and gray and electric, everywhere sweeping and swaying and twisting and turning, as if life itself had taken a leap out of shadows into light.

Oh, an incredible day, and how narrowly he found it; how easily he could have missed. A turn to the right instead of the left, a different word spoken, a different person met and none of it could have happened. Sam could have been in another place. . . .

So, crosswind stood the De Havilland Tiger Moth, singing, canvas and wire and wood singing with propeller drafts and breezes (he could have been in the Army or the Navy or somewhere else, but wasn't, but wasn't, but wasn't) and like the fat larva of a moth the flying instructor heaved his body up from the cockpit in front. Up and over the side like the grub of a moth. Up and over it and out, stretching, releasing his parachute catch, and flexing his back. Standing then on the frost-burned grass, peeling off his leather helmet, plucking off his gloves, and Sam knew the meaning of that. Oh my God yes; Sam knew the meaning of that.

"All right, Collins. She's yours. Take her off."

Away walked the instructor—Evans, Flying Officer, Royal Australian Air Force—striding, never looking back. Away he went, and away he went, and away, as the world became larger than Sam had ever seen it.

So small the instructor became. So distant. So antlike in the vastness.

Oh, so alone was Sam, his spirit failing, his body failing, so alone in his little airplane about to leave the earth.

Now you fly, Sam. On your own, Sam. Now you fly solo. All your years have brought you to it. All your life has prepared you for it. All the dreaming and all the striving and all the inevitability. Now you fly on your own like Bert Hinkler in his little airplane; Hinkler lying dead in Italian mountains when you were fifteen years and nine months.

"Please, God," Sam said. "I need help."

Sam trembling; nerves in his legs shaking; his tongue swelling dry; a thunder in his ears growing as loud as his remembering.

"Why the Air Force?" Mum said. "Oh, Sam, would they take a widow's son? Oh, Sam, couldn't you find a safer job? What's wrong with the Army? What's wrong with being a soldier? At least on the ground you stand a chance."

"I'll be a pilot," Sam said, "or nothing. It's not being stubborn or selfish or silly. I'll be a pilot because that's why I got born in the first place."

"I've never heard such nonsense. Sam, what nonsense you speak."

"It's all I've ever heard. All my life. How to be a man. How to stiffen the lip. How to die because I'm free and everyone else is not. How to grow up to be a hero. So I'll be one."

"I don't know what you're saying, Sam. I don't know where your ideas come from."

"I'm not going to die with a bayonet in my guts. I'm going to die with a bit of dignity. I'm not going to bleed my guts out into the mud."

"Why the Air Force?" the officer said at the interview. "Why come here with a ninth-grade education and trade qualifications? A technical-school certificate for carpentry! What sort of academic equipment is that? Axman. Farmhand. Selling newspapers on the street aged eleven. Oh, lad, what kind of equipment is that? The requirements are advertised clearly in black and white. We've got college boys and university graduates lined up by the hundreds waiting months to begin their training. What promise do you offer that they're not giving us straight? You'd never handle the academic side of it and you're twenty pounds too light for your stature and height. You're too tall to make a gunner— we'd have to wind you into the turret by the inch. And you'd never make a navigator without the mathematics. Coming in here with stars in your eyes is not enough. You've not had the breaks, lad, at the right times of your life. No one's blaming you for it, no one's judging you for it, but facts are facts and have got to be faced. You're not pilot material. I assure you, you are not."

"I'll be a pilot and nothing else."

"Then you'll be nothing. We can take our pick from the elite of the nation. I'm sorry I have to be so blunt. That's where we find our pilots, from among the elite. That's what it takes."

"You'll take me," Sam said, "and I'll leave the others behind me. I'm telling *you* that."

"Why the Air Force?" the flying instructor said. "Who did you know, Collins? Who's your uncle on the Air Board? Whose influence got you into this outfit? Why not the Navy? Or the Red Cross? Or the Pioneer Corps? You're perfect for a wheelbarrow and hobnailed boots. Sixty students on course and what do they give me? A new kind of species with two left hands and four left feet."

But the instructor climbed out and plucked off his gloves and clearly said, "All right, Collins. She's yours. Take her off." And left Sam alone beneath a heaven of hard blue glass.

Oh, the shock.

Oh, the realization.

Oh, the enormity of it. An airplane in his hands and he had never driven a motorcar. Never ridden a motorcycle. Never controlled a single self-propelled mechanical object—and this one, with a solitary irreversible error, could take his life.

The cockpit drill. Will it ever be remembered? Will it ever be dragged up from the mists? You've recited the words, Sam, and mimed the actions until you know them like a parrot, until you perform them like a puppet, until they happen through your hands whether you know consciously or not. That's what they say about it—practice until actions are instinctive and things happen the right way even when you forget how to count. Recite them awake. Recite them asleep.

The instructor? An appalling awareness of his absence.

Like turning to speak in an empty house. Like losing Mum at a sale in a city shop when you're three and a half.

"Mummy, Mummy, Mummy. Where's my mummy?"

Struggling all ways. Oh, crying. Oh, crashing into huge people in the dark whose faces are a mile up in the light. "Where's my mummy?" Oh, the pain, the destitution, the fright.

The empty cockpit in front. The vast plain of frost-burned grass. God a million miles high in the light. Nowhere is the instructor.

You're alone, Sam—all the universe and its laws are against you, banked up—joy stick in one hand, throttle in the other, rudder bar juddering like a kite string at your feet. The instruments of your own destruction at your own command for you to administer yourself. Six hours fifty minutes of instruction. Does that make you a pilot? How much longer did it take you to crawl in your cot?

Oh, sitting in a huddle, hunching up, shrinking out of sight; disappearing into caves, burrowing deep into the earth, deeper and deeper looking for warm brown safe earth. . . . There is no security. There is nowhere to go. There is no escape. Mum is somewhere else.

A light shines on you, Sam, green and apart, as if it had no source, shining across the grass. *Go*, says the light. Turn into wind, open your throttle, and *go*, says the light. Are you not a pilot? If in doubt throw a leg over the side and get out and give someone else a chance.

Hard blue sky and frost-burned grass and emptiness and fright and a disembodied green light. But you want to die with dignity. No bayonet for Sam. No stenching in ditches with your guts spilled out.

Swinging into wind, weathercocking around, noises in the

propeller like tiny fireworks, a quivering in the wing tips as if feathers fluttered, into wind swung the De Havilland Tiger Moth.

Go, Sam.

Oh, the disgrace if the instructor comes walking back, all the way back, striding larger and larger.

Why the Air Force, Collins, they'd say, when they drummed him out. Why do this to the people who want only to make a man of you, to the people who gave you a chance against every inclination of better judgment. There's a war to be won, boy. You'd better let proper men get on with the winning of it. We told you you'd not be good enough. We told you that pilots were made of special stuff.

Oh God, roaring blindly across the grass, so blindly, in blind defiance.

There was a fog in the sky, a fog in his brain, a fog in his vision. Everywhere black and white and gray, everywhere electric, everywhere sweeping and swaying and twisting and turning, and the instructor coming alongside the fuselage, gripping the rim of the cockpit with knuckles white and sharp.

"Very good, young Sam. Very good indeed. An excellent first solo. You're going to make a pilot. How about that?"

Oh, stunning the realization.

Oh, stunning the day, always separate, always in a box with edges of black and white. . . .

Over the mountains as if you were reading a story of breathless exploration, all the way over them, through the valleys and the villages, snow getting thicker. Hours it took them to pass round the hazards. Men with axes and crosscut saws swinging back and forth with beautiful motion, with noises

like dancers and rhythms like drumbeats. Draft horses and
farm horses, where men were not strong enough, dragging on
chains shifting tree trunks, steam spurting from their nos-
trils as if dragons were in season and St. George was expected. Children pitching snowballs and shrieking inanely
and making snowmen with hats on and buttons on their bel-
lies just as you saw in English comic books. Could it possibly
be the country he had grown up in?

"Oh, gee whiz, Mr. Hopgood. Once in seven years."

"No, Sam. Once in a lifetime. I've seen nothing like it
ever."

It was exhausting. You know? It fair wore him out.

"Would you like a cheese sandwich, Mr. Hopgood?"

"Yes, I would. Thank you very much."

There was no snow beside the sea that day. There never
had been as far as I know; not since the Ice Age, anyway.

Fourteen

"OPEN THE gate, Sam," Mr. Hopgood said, "and shut it securely after you. We don't leave gates open here. Then follow me down."

The motor truck drove through. It wasn't a Wolseley or
a Chrysler either. He had thought it might have been a
Bean. Would you believe! It was a Talbot. All that time deliberately not looking and there it was, suddenly seen. About
a 1910 chassis from the kind of guess that Sam made. No
wonder he hadn't known. *Talbot* it said on the front as it
went chugging through.

Sam shut the gate, securely, and followed on down along the tire tracks in the snow, followed quickly, because he had a sudden and irrational fear of being left behind. Stupid, because he was on the inside of the gate with the house in view.

It was a farm. A real farm. On a hillside surrounded by dark forest trees and cloud racing through with gloomy distances opening up for moments like snapshots. With plants looking like sticks standing in rows, and a paddock of dull green cabbages and streaks of snow and dark brown soil in between, with lots of hens somewhere making a terrible noise, with a whinnying draft horse and two bellowing cows, and a wildly bleating billy goat on a chain and two black watchdogs scorching up and down running wires and barking fit to choke. With a curious-looking "home-made" house of unpainted split timbers growing out of the ground and heavily patched corrugated iron water tanks tucked under the eaves and a strange chimney, pyramid-shaped, built of round stones and masses of mud mortar or cement turned brown. With violets; little violets on clumpy bushes beside the path—purple in the snow—and rose bushes and wattle trees and shrubs covered in large red flowers that looked luminous and liquid against the snow. With a barn, at least Sam supposed it to be a barn, into which Mr. Hopgood drove. No walls, none at all, just a roof that went on and on and on, bending and bowing, rising and falling, held up on tree trunks thicker than grown men. Gee, the things that were in it, huddling out of the cold. Hundreds and hundreds of things in the gloom, in the deep shadows, everything looking black, everything just shapes. The first ploughs Sam had ever seen up close. Beautiful they were. All sorts of rusty things with rusty iron wheels. Bellows—and what had to be a forge. A real forge, as in a blacksmith's shop, with a cylindrical piece of steel swinging from a beam, for hitting perhaps, for making ringing sounds. And horseshoes everywhere on thick rusty nails. And more spades and shovels and picks and forks and rakes and hoes than Sam had ever counted in one place before, all with handles made of young sapling trees, smooth, dimpled, and almost straight. Stacks and stacks of nuts and bolts tied in bundles and coils of wire and rope and bits of engines and scrap metal and harness for horses and axes and planks and boxes and bags and pipes and chains and bicycle frames and animal traps and leather straps and hammers and iron spikes and spanners, the BIGGEST spanners Sam had ever seen, and wooden cartwheels and rubber motor tires and barrels and bins and tins and oh my goodness just about everything that ever was since the world began. Like opening a chest in a secret room and finding in it real treasures, not just useless jewels. But such a strange building, such a strange shape. Had someone planted a seed and lovingly watered it and watched it grow like a huge-leafed pumpkin vine over humps and hillocks and hollow trees? That was how it seemed to be.

Someone was standing there. Standing beyond, as if she had run uphill and stopped suddenly. Was it a woman or a girl? With a bucket in hand? He couldn't see her features; couldn't determine her age; just knew with a feeling of slight unease, of slight unreality, that she was there, that she had stopped running because of him, because of Sam. Like everything else, she was not much more than a shape in the heavy light— light that yielded up detail only when you stared. Then she was gone. Disappeared. Perhaps she ducked down or turned into a breeze or was never there at all in fact and flesh. At the house a door opened and a woman seemed to form out of pieces of light. She stepped to the ground, but saw Sam, and paused. It was strange. Well, it was strange to Sam.

"Come on, boy," Mr. Hopgood said. "You must be ready for a cup of tea."

Sam felt scared.

"This is Sam," Mr. Hopgood said, "and this is my wife, Mrs. Hopgood, and that's Sally Hopgood over there out of sight round the corner, being silly. Don't believe she's shy, Sam, or dumb either. She's got more to say than anyone I know. And don't imagine she's out of hearing—she's got rabbit ears. Where's Bernie? Not down the shaft *today*. I hope he's got the pump going; I can't hear it; have you been to see? Maud, I've told him, I've told you, when it's wet, when it rains, you don't work the shaft. I don't care what anyone says. I don't care if he's struck a vein of gold a foot through. What's gold, for God's sake! I met Sam on the road. Just as well. Helped me shift the trees. Five or six we had to shift before we got to Belgrave. After that the gangs were out. If I'd not had Sam you mightn't have seen me till midnight. That's the difference; another pair of hands. *Sally! There's bacon in the truck. Bring it through.* Come on, Sam."

Oh, it was strange. And so was Mr. Hopgood. He was a different man.

"What do you think of the snow? Really something, wouldn't you say? I reckon it's twenty years since we've seen anything to compare. When Linda was being born. That drive in the sulky to Lilydale. Lord, what a drive. Hope it hasn't killed the passionfruit. What a year to put them in, three hundred vines, so it snows. Have you been down to see? The eucalypts can't stand it. Trees breaking everywhere. Just breaking from strain. I saw the bough of a messmate down that must have been a foot and a half through. Good sound timber, snapped clean. It was in my mind coming home. All the way. Maybe the next one to snap will land across Sam and me. Any one of ten thousand trees hanging over us as we came through. Beautiful mess that would have been. God was merciful, for a change. It's a nice bit of bacon. Couldn't let it pass. *Sally, under the seat, wrapped in newspaper.* It'll give us a rest from mutton stew. They were practically giving it away. Same as cabbages. Left them with the hospital again. What's the point of it any more? Do you know? I don't. All that time. All that effort. Six months growing in the ground. And what for?"

(Moving they were, Mr. Hopgood and Sam, all the time, across the open ground, skirting round the woman, through the door, sitting down inside.)

"They're not buying, Maud. Just not buying. God knows what people are eating when you can't sell cabbages. Bringing home cabbages like those in weather like this. Real value for money; beautiful cabbages like those. Not a bid they gave me. Not a bid did I hear. 'I'm giving them to you,' I said at the hospital, 'free. Free, for God's sake; forty dozen cabbages again. Yes,' I said, 'the man from last week back again, remember me? Eighty dozen cabbages I've cut for market this season. That's eighty dozen cabbages I've brought here. When I'm sick I can't afford hospitals, I can't afford doctors, my wife calls up the spirits. Look, I'll even carry them into your kitchen rather than chuck 'em away. Beautiful cabbages like these.' All that care bringing them into the world, but I suppose there's a limit to what they can use even when they get 'em free. Loosen your boots, Sam. No prizes for suffering, boy."

The woman stood against the open doorway; from the inside silhouetted against the light out there of dark clouds racing and white snow lying as still as stones. She was a

large woman, heavy fleshed but not gross, and had not ut-
tered a word, and had scarcely glanced at Sam. She was
larger than Mr. Hopgood—oh, by quite a deal. Twice as big,
maybe, though it was hard to say. Was he frightened of her?
All those words tumbling round with hardly a breath in
between?

"So you didn't sell the cabbages? Not even a couple of
dozen to pay your expenses? And you used all that petrol
to get to Melbourne and to get back home again. And you
had to pay for breakfast—or go without. And pay for the
bacon. And pay for everything else you walked on and sat
on, as well as your market stand. And of the money you took
with you, how much have you brought home? Don't tell me,
Jack Hopgood, I know. And you carried the cabbages yourself, inside, to give away. And you say this is Sam. Who's
Sam?"

"Sam needs a friend," Jack Hopgood said, "and you'd have
no more left him there than I. Fix us some tea, sweetheart.
It's been a long hard day. We're frozen. We're starved."

No. The man wasn't frightened of her. Perhaps they were
blind angry with the world, but not with each other. Maybe
they wanted to scream and shout and beat their fists against
the wall, and were finding another way. It was terrible being
a kid at times. It was terrible being a grownup, too. Then in
came Sally with the bacon in her hands.

Fifteen

OH, SALLY, what matters when there's someone in the world
like you? What matters, Sally? Nothing, nothing, nothing.

Oh, have you stopped to look at yourself? As I see you? In the soft light, so soft in here, not heavy like outside; everything soft and delicate rather than vague. Everything dreamy; so dreamy, Sally, that it's hard to say where the real you stops and the bits I make up carry on. I don't know.

Oh, Sally, I don't know why you are, or where you're from, or what, but I'm in the world because of you. That's why I'm here—I just never, never knew before. I can see tomorrow real clear, and there you are with me. Did you know?

Little Rose and grown-up Rose and everything round about and in between were only saying that one day I'd wake up and there you'd be. What's been saying it to you, Sally? Have you been hearing there'd be me?

I feel strange.

I thought grown-up Rose was the one; that's what went wrong with the day. Today being the day. Today's the day, Sally. Today. Today.

There she was looking beautiful with her hair in the wind and the rain beating down. Can you blame me for mistaking her, for thinking she was you? Though you're not like her, no way at all. How could you be? Rose being married, just to start with, just for starters, being married an' all. I think she meant to be kind though, don't you? But fancy taking my money that way. What a thing to do. If she hadn't, though, I'd not have found you. The way things go. The way it is. I'd have gone on looking yet for years and years and years, being lost and not knowing why, not knowing I hadn't arrived at you. Or would I have got there by some other road?

Do you have lights in here? We need them, Sally. I can't see you, not properly, not in the way I want to. I feel strange.

I don't like things being so soft, so dreamy, so hard to see. Just little pictures I keep putting together wondering whether they're really you. But I know you're there and I know you're the one and I know it's me for you. Because I can still see tomorrow, so clear, and Sally's the name that keeps coming out of there.

All the things that have brought me here.

Old Mo in the ticket box playing his game. Maybe he's an angel down from heaven on holidays. Maybe today he sells tickets and tomorrow he goes to the races and the day after he's archbishop somewhere. Everything. Everything that's happened. If the guard hadn't given me tuppence and told me where to go. If the lady hadn't been feeding her baby I'd have caught that train. If the lavatory hadn't been so smelly I'd have gone back in again—and sat there, and waited. I suppose.

It it hadn't snowed. If your dad hadn't pulled in to the side of the road. If he'd sold his cabbages and gone straight home. If he'd not planted them at all. If he'd gone to market tomorrow instead of today.

Sally, all these things happening, one by one, just for bringing me to you and you to me. Think of the organization behind the scenes. Think of the bookwork: God working overtime.

If I hadn't hit the tram, I ask you, where would I be?

If Mr. Vale had fixed me brakes one more time.

If I'd not been riding in that rotten rain.

If I'd not been dreaming and singing a tune.

If it had not been slippery when I jammed me back wheel.

If I'd shot past the tram down the other side.

If those *Herald*s hadn't been ruined on the road.

Take one *if* out and I'd be delivering my *Herald*s now.

Delivering them today. Sixty-four *Herald*s on me old bike balanced across the bar. That's what your clock says, Sally, if I'm seeing it at all—half-past four. At half-past four since I was eleven years old I've been shooting down Riversdale Road. I'd be shooting down Riversdale now.

Hey, Sally. It's twenty-four hours since I hit the tram. You don't even know that—what's brought me here. In twenty-four hours I arrive at you. Gee.

If I'd hit the tram today, everything would have been different. I wouldn't even have seen the snow.

Sally, I feel strange. Oh Sally, I think something's wrong with me.

"Oh, Mr. Hopgood. Mr. Hopgood. Please . . ."

Sixteen

VOICES WERE there, drifting across the frontier of consciousness, and nothing was going on inside Sam now to keep the meaning out. But when the voices actually happened was hard to say. Maybe they had happened before, whenever that might have been, because Sam was certain he was looking at the people and their lips were not matching up. Yeh—it was an experience—it was "off the edge" again. Mrs. Hopgood's voice was clear, was unmistakable, it just had to be, though she was standing at the stove stirring at a black pot, her lips making no movement at all.

"It's terrible, Jack. I've never seen a boy faint away, never seen anyone faint away like it. You're far too casual. Far too cavalier."

Mr. Hopgood appeared to be sitting at the edge of a long settee, probably a hard one, looking haggard, looking worried, but not saying a word, yet his voice filled the room. "This is not an emergency. I've told you, it's exhaustion. There's nothing wrong with the boy."

"Picking up strangers, Jack. You never think ahead. You know nothing about him."

"I don't need to know anything about him. I can see for myself."

"Murders and terrible things happening everywhere. Bringing him into our house. Bringing him here and expecting him to stay. He could be riddled with disease. He could be mental. I don't like the way he was staring at Sally. He could be violent. He looks so—so vague."

"Oh, make up your mind. One thing or the other. He can't be everything at the same time."

"Well, he looks like a half-wit to me, if you must know, looks like a defective to me. You keep away from him, Sally. I'd be happier if you left the room; if you stayed away, if you stayed right out of sight until we send him packing. You've been warned. You watch him. Don't give him an inch. They're cunning, you know. They're as cunning as foxes."

"This is silly, Maud. He's a nice boy. The boy's all right."

"You've seen the state he's in! Do nice people get knocked about like that? Looks to me as though he's been restrained. Looks to me as though he's been in a strait-jacket. Didn't he tell you about it? Didn't you notice the state he was in? All that time with him and you never even noticed? I find it hard to believe that anyone could shut his eyes to these things. Jack, you do take chances. Bringing him here. We're so isolated. Where do we turn for help? There could be a price on his head."

"Oh, for heaven's sake. One mere boy and four of us."

"They turn violent with the strength of ten men; you know that. And there's nothing on him to give a clue. Not a thing. Sam's his name, you say. Sam from where? Sam who?"

"He's half-starved. There's nothing else wrong with him."

"He had sandwiches, didn't he? You said so yourself. You told me you ate one of them. Lucky you weren't poisoned. You're inconsistent. Since when have you taken food from starving children? Healthy people don't faint. Healthy boys never faint. He's probably diabetic. He's probably consumptive. And he had money in his pocket. Tenpence in his pocket. Stolen from where? Probably more than you brought home. Not picked from *your* pocket, I suppose? I've told you, Sally, go to your room, and until we've got to the bottom of this, stay there. He's probably escaped from a lunatic asylum or a reform school or a sanatorium. He's probably been on the run for days, stealing from people as he goes."

"He's a clean, healthy, nice boy. He was beautiful in the snow."

"Beautiful? What an extraordinary word!"

"Because it's the only word. Because I saw him in the snow and you didn't. He was in a state of joy."

"Now you're being feeble, Jack. People in a 'state of joy' can cut your throat twenty minutes later."

"Every mile of the way. He made something special of it, of every turn of the road. I've never seen these hills as this boy made me see them. I don't care about the passionfruit vines. I'm sorry they're gone, sorry we've lost them, sorry I've failed again, they should have been protected and the fault's mine, but to have spent this afternoon with Sam is a fair exchange."

"You sound pathetic."

"I am not pathetic and there's nothing wrong with Sam that a bellyful of good food and a night in a good bed won't fix. I'm sure he can hear us. I'm sure he can hear every word you say. Have some consideration for his feelings, please."

"Hearing is not understanding, Jack. He looks foreign, anyway. Bless me, I wish him no harm, but I'm not wishing for harm to be brought upon us either."

Three people were there, but the third wasn't Sally. The third was a youth of about eighteen or nineteen, lightly built and small. He was sitting on a wooden bench with his back to the wall, drinking from a large brown mug with steam in the air. "I reckon we should dig upstream," he said, but that didn't make sense to Sam, and the voice had about it a different sound, as if spoken now instead of at another time. "I reckon that's the way we should drive."

"You'll go in the direction I've marked and nowhere else. And you'll never swing another pick in that shaft on a wet day. Bernie, I'm surprised at you. The gully's full of streams, full of streams, as you know. More below the surface deep down than above the ground and running like mad when there's rain. You know. You know. You've been told. You're lucky to be alive."

"Oh, Dad."

"Having brought you in one piece to the present age is a miracle around here as far as I'm concerned, and I'm not proposing to lose the struggle now."

"He's hearing us, Dad. I reckon he is. I reckon he's looking at you."

A kerosene lamp was burning yellow in the room and the window glass behind the net curtain was a black hole as if night had come down. It was like being in a cave; a very strange room. Rough-hewn. Timbers in the roof with ax marks on them. That huge funnel-shaped fireplace made of smooth round stones and a square iron cooking stove just like Mum's at home. A trestle table made of planks and scrubbed honey-gold. Tapestry chairs, threadbare and worn, with upholstered wooden arms, and wooden benches for sitting on along the wall. And a settee; a long, hard settee of faded tapestry and horsehair upon which Sam was laid, a pillow under his head. Mr. Hopgood seated in such a way that Sam could not roll off or fall.

Sam didn't know what to say. If that was what the lady thought of him, he'd have to go. But he didn't feel strong enough or well enough and it was nighttime out there. Nighttime and snow on the ground.

"Are you all right, dear?" Mrs. Hopgood said. "You've had us very worried, you know."

Sam shook his head.

"What does that mean?"

Sam shook his head.

"Sit him up, Jack. Prop him up. Bernie, get Sam another cushion. Here you are, dear. A nice bowl of stew and there's plenty more. Do you want some help, dear? Can you manage on your own? Then it's straight to bed for you."

Sam's eyes filled with tears.

He didn't understand.

But Sally truly wasn't in the room and could not be seen.

Seventeen

PERHAPS IT was a better awakening than the day before, at first warm, anyway, and clean, though something struck against his stretching leg at the bottom of the bed; a hot-water bottle gone cold. Probably a fellow could put up with that—but down there the whole bed was as shockingly cold as the air that had struck him when he had stepped from the train. Sam drew his foot back up again in alarm.

He was lost and insecure, that was how it seemed, and all the reasons were gathering inside him like a swarm. Putting the reasons together wasn't hard. Together they came, a dark and brooding and overwhelming swarm. What terrible things she had said about him, terrible things, terrible—no matter how she had fussed over him later, or fed him, or got him to bed, no matter how or what had happened then, the damage had been done before. It still made him want to cry, even now, with a whole night in between—to have been called names of that kind. To be called names. Words hurt more than sticks and stones and trams.

It was light again. A window over there was looking gray, looking like day. Piece by piece the room took shape, as though once a girl had lived there, but not now. Perhaps a girl who had gone away. It was time, too, for Sam to go. To get up out of this bed and quietly dress and go.

Go where? Go where? Decisions again today. Who would make them this time? Someone else—or Sam?

It was awful about Sally, such a shame, but in ten years' time he'd return. He'd return and say, "Here I am, Sally. Back again. I remembered every day. All these years I've been coming home to you, every day. I'm not bad, Sally. I'm not mad, Sally. I'm not any of those things your mother said. I'm just me, Samuel Spencer Collins, famous pilot, the very same, first to fly nonstop across the Poles. It was in all the papers (in the *Herald*, too) and on the newsreels. You must have seen. Years ago I was here on the day it snowed and they sent you to your room so you'd not be polluted, so you'd not catch a disease. Samuel Spencer Collins, the very same. They thought I was unconscious, or asleep, or stupid, or foreign, I think I heard, I heard, I heard every word. I wish I hadn't though."

I'm hungry again, too. Like a lion. What am I supposed to do? Everything out there is so cold, so strange. I suppose the snow's got deeper now. And deeper and deeper now. I suppose I'll sink to my waist or sink out of sight and drown. Drown in snow. Oh my gawd. Nowhere to swim. Nowhere to see. Nowhere to go. I'll lose my way and perish, you know. Though how can you lose your way when you have nowhere to go? Everything being so cold. Where will I buy a pie up here? There wouldn't be a pie shop in fifty miles. Where would I buy a potato cake like I get at Joe's? They're probably not invented here. I'll have to eat the leaves off the trees. Maybe if I waited for breakfast, hey, and then slipped away? Nice and sunny on the Murray, they reckon. It's where I should have gone, you know. That blooming old Mo. Sending me to Fern Tree Gully. Sending me to the snow! I mean to say—who ever heard of it, of snow!

Fancy saying I was defective like something that's not properly made. Fancy saying I was diseased. Poor old Pete's a diabetic; that's a word she used. Poor old Pete. Surely people don't think about him that way. It's not even fair. Diseased? It's a terrible, horrible word. Like saying you're dirty or something. Like saying you smell. Like saying you're unclean, like pigs in a stinking sty. Fancy sending Sally away as if I was going to turn her bad, like something rotten, if she breathed my air in the room.

I want my mum.

No, I don't. I take it back. I don't want my mum at all. I'm sorry, Mum; no offense; but I'm fourteen and a half now.

Less a few days. Of course I don't want my mum. I don't
want my dad either. I don't want anybody. Gawd, I sure
don't want my auntie. And blooming little Rose can get lost
up a drain or down a hole. (Terrible little kid she is, running
me ragged all these years.) I bet Sally would kiss me though,
if they gave her half a chance. I bet Sally would hold my
hand. Blooming little Rose egging me on all those years and
never giving me a cuddle even. The stories my cousins tell
about their girls; they live in another world, I reckon. Fourteen and a half I am and never been kissed fair and square.
I must be the oldest kid alive who can say it. I had me chance
yesterday though, I suppose I did, I suppose; and I bally well
ran away. I suppose I'll end up being a hermit in a cave. I suppose I'm one of those kids who'll never have the nerve. I'm
as big a jelly as little Rose. They'll stick it on me grave. *Here
he lies, as pure as driven snow. Not meaning to be, but from
sheer lack of nerve.* I've got to go. I've just got to get out of
here.

"Sam."

Mr. Hopgood it was, standing at the door, with a shaving
brush in hand, and a frown, and lather round his face like a
white beard at Christmas time.

"Yes, sir," said Sam.

"Have you slept?"

"Yes, sir."

"Feeling better now?"

"I think so, sir."

"Do you want to stay in bed?"

"No, sir."

"You may if you wish. There's no hurry. There's nothing
much to do outside. The fog's so thick out there it's like being
under the sea."

"I'll get up, sir. If you don't mind. Please."

"I don't mind, Sam. It's up to you. You're quite well?"

"Yes, sir. . . . Of course I am. . . . Of course I am. . . . Quite well every way. There's nothing wrong with me. I've never been to a doctor except for wax in my ears, and I've never been in a hospital, except to get born. I've never been sick for more than a day. I've had the measles. I've had the chicken pox. I've had a cold in my nose. And I got run over by a tram. That's all that happened to me. I got run over by a tram. That's where me bruises come from. From a bloomin' tram. A bloomin' great tram. It's a wonder it didn't kill me. And me bike got busted and I lost me papers all over the road. All over the road in the rain. People pickin' 'em up and takin' 'em away. People pinchin' my papers. Cars drivin' over 'em. Everythin' gettin' muddied and torn. I took the money though. I shouldn't have done that. I took the small change and someone stole it from me, which served me right I suppose. And I'm all on my own. And I can't go home because how can Mum pay for sixty-four *Heralds*? And I can't go to Mr. Lynch because he'll call me a thief and take my job away. And everyone's out of work at our house. And Pete. Poor Old Pete. He'll die. It's not nice callin' him diseased, callin' him dirty. And with me not earning any money what happens about his special food? Why's it all such a muddle? Why's it all so cruel? Oh, Mr. Hopgood, there's nothing wrong with me. True. True. True. I got run over by a tram and Rose frightened me, making a pass at me. I got stuck under that rotten church; that's what happened to me. I got stuck there and couldn't get free. I've never been sick in my life and I wouldn't hurt your Sally. I'd never hurt your Sally. If anyone hurt her I'd kill 'em, honest I would. True."

"Hey, hey, hey."

The man was sitting on the bed, holding Sam to him, holding him and rocking him back and forth, and Mrs. Hopgood's voice was somewhere in the room.

"I'm sorry, Sam. Oh, I'm sorry, Sam. I could cut out my evil tongue. Of course you're a good boy. I should have known."

Eighteen

SALLY WAS at breakfast. In the broad daylight there she was. Well, in daylight as broad as the fog allowed. Sitting across that scrubbed table, that honey-colored table, set with red flowers from the snow, and buttered toast heaped up, and oatmeal porridge, and in a tall brown jug new milk so thick it looked like cream, and golden marmalade made from oranges and lemons growing on the hill outside, and egg cups standing in a row. Everyone was waiting for Sam.

"Sit there, Sam."

Oh, Sally, I see you there. And this is me—if you'll take a look at me. You're different close up from the picture I'd made.

"Sally," Mr. Hopgood said, "this is Sam. Of course you know, but you've not had a chance to say hullo. You should have things in common, you two; both going on fifteen. When's your birthday, Sam?"

"Third of April, sir."

"Sally's is the twelfth of June."

Bernie was looking smug, as if he knew. He was small like

his dad, and didn't have much to say, or else he was as hungry as Sam. In daylight he looked smaller than the night before. Strange, you know, when you considered the food. It should have built bodies ten feet tall.

"Sally, say the blessing, please."

Sam closed his eyes and listened to her voice.

Oh, you could hear sunshine in it. You could hear clouds and mist in the morning leaves. You could hear snow falling and the moon rising. You could hear wings stretching and flowers opening and Mrs. Hopgood saying, "Sam."

"Yes, ma'am."

"Your breakfast."

Food? Who wanted food, when Sally was sitting there. Her hair rested on her shoulders as if pausing for a while. It was red. A complete surprise. I mean *red*, like carrots or roofing tiles. As red as hair could be. He had expected it to be black or brown or gold maybe. And she had freckles. More freckles to the inch than Sam had ever seen. And eyes so blue. Oh, the blue so blue and the white so white—eyes so brilliant he could hardly breathe. She was like a color picture; honest; as if the artist had painted it stark and clear with colors straight from the tube. When she glanced his way his heart stopped beating. It did, you know. Dropped. Stopped. Seized up. As if it would never start again. As if his time had come to die. Then it hammered at his ribs like the fist of an iron man breaking down a door.

Sam couldn't look back again. He simply didn't dare. How *could* he look again into those eyes, into those deep clear pools—while other people were around? Never, while other people were talking about the fog and the snow that had all but gone from the ground and Sally was nodding and smiling and saying "um" or "how?" or "where?" and Bernie was looking *so* smug now—not unkindly though—as if he knew everything that was happening inside Sam. Well, not that Sam himself was sure. There were express trains inside, traveling in opposite directions, screaming through station after station with their whistles blowing.

The porridge was strange, so strange. Beautiful to look at, beautiful to stroke with the spoon—once a fellow knew it was there, once his vision cleared! Different from Mum's porridge; quite, quite different; porridge such as Sam had never tasted, never seen. Fascinating. Thick brown sugar in it made marble stains with the spoon; back and forth with the spoon, round and round. Was it really for eating? Seriously, I mean. Maybe you should model things out of it—heads or airplanes—and afterward would it set solid like stone?

Mr. Hopgood poured glasses of milk; one for Sally, one for Bernie, one for Sam. Yellow milk, not white with lots of water in it as Sam was used to at home, not "liquid" in the usual sense of the word, milk that lurched sluggishly in the glass and went down so thickly, so smoothly, that it worried Sam and anxiously he had to edge the glass away because he thought of Pete living on food so weak it almost fell over from sheer fatigue, because he wasn't sure if ordinary kids with ordinary stomachs could hold the stuff down, and being sick yesterday, being sick once was enough for Sam. And it would be frightful to be sick in this house, because they might put Sally in another room, and Sam wanted Sally as close to him as she could be. Was the fragrance in the air Sally or the flowers?

"Sam, does your mother know?"

"Does she know what, ma'am?"

"Where you've been? What you've done? Where you've arrived?"

What a stupid thing to ask. How could she know when Sam hadn't got round to working it out for himself yet?

"No, ma'am."

Was Mr. Hopgood looking uncomfortable? Was he attending to his toast with a degree of concentration more suited to climbing a church steeple?

"Immediately after breakfast," Mrs. Hopgood said, "write her a letter, Sam, and Bernie can post it for you when he goes into town for the mail."

Sam's spirits went plunging again, plunging down.

"People will be looking for you now. If you had an accident with a tram it will be known. In the newspapers perhaps, and the police will have been informed. People will be terribly concerned for you. Perhaps people already are wondering if you're wandering about confused or have met with foul play."

"I don't think so."

"Oh yes, Sam."

"But if I write a letter they'll read the postmark and know where I am."

"That's right, Sam."

Couldn't she see? Couldn't she understand that there came a time when a boy had to go it alone? Maybe not boys like Bernie, but boys like Sam. Surely it was sticking out a mile?

"But I don't want them to know. That'll spoil it all. I've got to have a say myself in what I do."

"Running away is a terrible thing, Sam. Have you thought of the people you've left at home? Of how they feel? Does your family love you?"

Sam dropped his eyes and felt a big pain, with Mum there in the middle of it.

"Well, do they?"

"Yes, ma'am."

"And do you love them?"

"Of course I do."

"Well your duty is plain."

"What's duty got to do with it?" He shook his head, though he was seeing it so clearly now, and feeling it strongly. They had to understand he didn't spend his life sobbing in people's arms. "It's because I love my family that I've gone away."

"They may find it difficult to believe."

"They'll work it out, ma'am. Mum's pretty quick on the uptake. I reckon she'd have got round to it in double quick time."

"Well, tell her she's right then. Have some pity on her. She'll be sick with worry, worrying about you. If you love her, you've got to, Sam."

"She knows I can look after myself."

"When you've been run over by a tram?"

"Well, I have looked after myself, haven't I? So far. And I didn't ask Mr. Hopgood for a ride, did I? He asked me to come, didn't you, Mr. Hopgood, and I'm very grateful, ma'am, but Mum knows I'm all right. I've been selling papers for three years. I'm the senior boy on the rounds. I'm responsible, I am. I can make up my own mind."

"Then you must stay on with us until you decide what you're going to do. You must tell your mother that also, then she'll really know. I think it would be best if I put a note about it at the bottom of the page. Nothing special; just a little note in an adult hand."

Oh, she was cunning. Not like Auntie, but sneaky just the same. There'd be no blank sheet of paper in the envelope—or false trails. Mum would have known if she had seen his handwriting on the envelope; that would have been enough to tell her he was safe and alive; but now his letter would be read and certified. Honest, how could you win against them? If you shook one off, another arose. It was like living in a jar on display. If you forced the lid up a bit for a moment someone else screwed it down.

He looked to Mr. Hopgood with abject appeal. He must have understood. He must have known. But his eyes were averted as if the matter were out of his hands.

"Eat up, Sam," Mrs. Hopgood said. "You'll need your strength later in the day. If it's fine when Bernie comes back from the mail, you can help him dig for gold."

Sally went off to school. Sam was so surprised.

"Good-by, Such. Good-by, Dave," Sally called to the watchdogs running up and down the wires.

Bernie got his bike out to go for the mail and Sally got her bike out and away they rode together. Peculiar-looking bikes they were, too, as if they were homemade.

"Good-by, Thicket," Sally called to the goat tugging on his chain.

Sam followed hopefully to the gate at the road, like a hound hoping for a pat on the head, but Sally and Bernie took more notice of the cows leaning over the fence from the paddock at the side. "Good-by, Belinda. Good-by, Katie," Sally called.

There had never been anyone in Sam's school like Sally. If there had been he would not have left home. Wow—and if Sally had lived a few doors away instead of little Rose! Twenty-four girls in his class last year, but not one of them would he have wanted to kiss if they had given you a prize. Well, maybe Harry Thompson or Julie Rhodes if you could have shut your eyes. This year, would you believe, the whole class was boys. Sam had thought—without thinking about it —that Sally would have been working at home like most other girls of her age. Maybe she was slow and still in a lower grade.

All day she'd be away. All day she'd be gone. How could he wait around for seven whole hours? Away they rode, the two of them, into fog that swallowed them up, and Sally didn't even wave.

Sam had not spoken a single word to her. Just like Bernie she was. Tongue-tied. Neither of them with a word to say, except to their parents, or to goats or dogs or cows. Sally didn't seem to care if he was dead or alive. But that, after all, was the way girls were supposed to be when they were interested in a boy. There was a ritual to be observed—or so the kids reckoned who knew anything about the game.

It was a shame she had gone. Well, he'd be back for her in ten years.

Sam looked quickly toward the house. Nothing was there; nothing was to be seen but fog drawn like a screen across the world.

Sam opened the gate a foot or two, stepped through, and ran off along the road in the opposite direction to "town." It was bad, going without his overcoat, but he'd never slip back to get it without betraying his move. At least he had tenpence in his pocket and a full belly and a clean getaway.

He had forced it upon himself, this having to go and having to leave Sally behind, though he'd take her with him always—he knew that—in his mind. Pretty poor substitute though, just thinking about it. Fancy getting wound up again like a Gramophone and blurting out too much. Always the same. Always telling tales on myself I am. I must be soft in the skull. Why do I go rattling on when I know I'm doing myself down? I mean, I could have kissed her, I know I could have, I know I would have, I just know. Might have taken a week or two, but I just know. And it would have been pretty good digging for gold. I might have found some, who knows, and then sixty-four *Herald*s wouldn't have mattered and Mum could have stopped worrying for a change.

There was a call from somewhere, a muffled sound, as if things were wrapped around it. "Sam. . . . Don't be foolish. . . ."

Leaving Mr. Hopgood behind was also a shame.

Nineteen

GIPPSLAND was in the east somewhere, the wide land, and Sam reckoned east was *that* way, just as it had been when he had run from grown-up Rose. It was hard to say for sure in a world so fog-bound; but he was going farther, he was heading away from home into the wide land; the feeling was in his bones; you know?

It was very cold. Here and there, against tussocks of wire grass at the roadside, were icy-looking residues of snow, and masses of bushes, all kinds of rough and tangled bushes, mainly with yellow flowers drooping heavy with dew or rain. Sam needed his overcoat; oh, he needed it badly, and he hurried, hoping to keep warm, hoping to raise a sweat, but there were areas of stiffness inside him, and there were bruises leaving an awareness in him (like a voice) of pain. And the air was raw, like a wound, and hurt his nose and burned his throat and tightened his lungs disturbingly. Was it cloud, thick cloud, not fog at all? Was he way up high where oxygen was rare? Who could say? From looking around you'd never know. Or was it all upside down? Had he crossed a line and passed beneath the sea? It's like the sea out there, Mr. Hopgood had said.

In the deep ocean—that's where he could have been—with huge agglomerations of weed lying eerily lit and stagnant in the gloom, or almost stagnant, stirring just enough to let you know they were alive out there. He didn't like it at all—though he knew it couldn't be true.

Oh, it was different from fog at home. There were lights in the fog at home; lights making beautiful patterns, turning into stars, turning into gods or angels shimmering about with rays. And you were never far from Wickham Street, from Mum's kitchen stove. Or else you were on your way to school with kids around, and you'd get inside, in the warm cheer, and sit on the hot-water radiators against the classroom walls, hands tucked under your thighs, glad to be there; a special day because there was fog outside. Not like here.

Here there were no lights because it was the wrong time of day, unless lights grew in trees or hung from clouds. And there were no people around, no human presence, no voices, no kids to make the place real, no feeling of surety that a healthy yell would bring anyone to your aid except the Hopgoods or people the Hopgoods knew.

There was something unearthly about it, as if just off the edge of proper sight and sound and feel, as if by opening that gate he had obeyed an instinct that might not have been for ultimate good, as if by ignoring the call of his name he had broken another thread of life's cord. How many threads were left to break before the cord parted into separate ends and couldn't keep him alive any more? Maybe he had broken a few too many in the last couple of days. This feeling of being "off the edge" all the time, this knowing without thinking that you were running with blinkers on, that a journey begun had to go on to the end no matter what came in between . . .

What happened inside him when he hit the tram? Apart from bruising and jarrings and aches and pains. One day a fellow was a happy little soul—well, as happy and as little as a fellow can be at five feet eight inches tall and fourteen years of age—the next he was struggling with the secrets of the world and every mystery faced was the door to one mystery more. But he'd not go back. Oh no. He'd not go back to anything as it used to be. It was better knowing than not knowing. It was better to feel scared than not to feel at all.

Turning into Wickham Street. . . . Oh. . . . Oh. . . .

Everything had changed.

Oh, it was so different from before; everything had become small and aged; so different from 1931 (so long ago), so different from 1929 when he had come home so scared from blackberrying with Rose.

It made him sick, you know, and he had to pause.

Did Rose live there still? In that small brown house with paint flaking from the walls, with the door her father had slammed? She'd probably not know him now. He might not want to know her.

Fourteen Wickham Street. Mum, here I am.

Is this really where it all used to be?

It looks so small and run-down. Maybe it was always small and run-down. Maybe it only *looked* big before.

Mum, here I am. The prodigal returned.

The knocking on your door is me. Your Sam. I'm sorry it's all so posed, Mum, but there's no other way so live it through. Don't die, Mum. Don't drop dead from heart failure, Mum. Have you forgiven me? Here I am, waiting for you to answer my call.

There she stands, a snapshot in an old frame, turning very pale; and oh, so changed, so small down there, and tired and gray.

"Yes, Mum...."

He can hear her breath. It comes so sharp and short and loud.

"Yes, Mum. Oh, yes, Mum. . . . It's me. Oh, Mum, I've missed you. I've come home."

Oh, get a hold on her, Sam. Quickly, Sam. She needs your living arms. She needs to know it's still the boy who kissed her hair.

The next day in the shed outside she showed him the bicycle there. "It's been here four years, Sam. This man came about a month after you went away. Your dad had a few words with him but he never told me what they had to say. He came in an old truck with cabbages on the back. Dad was vague about his name. He'd made the bike for you, he said. He said you'd know."

Hurrying along that road, hurrying to keep warm in the fog and the shadows of melting snow. But when it's time, a boy has to go.

Sally, is this why you had nothing to say to me? You knew, you could see that for you and for Sam it was too late or too soon? Did you really know that this fellow Sam was going somewhere else, was going down a way that wasn't yours?

And you had to let him get on with it? Or were you so full
of other things that you didn't see at all?

Oh, Sally. (I didn't know.) Oh, Sally, after school that day
behind the blackwood tree, leaning there, oh leaning there
dazed, leaning there half-crazed, weeping for Bernie your
brother underground, Bernie digging his shaft upstream instead of the other way down, Bernie not hearing the ringing
of the steel cylinder hanging in the barn when three o'clock
came around, never hearing the call for afternoon tea ever
again. And Sam? Miles and miles and miles away by then,
discovering his world. Discovering more than he knew. Living out the years that would not have otherwise been.

Twenty

THE GENERAL store was at the end of a long, long, long
road. It wasn't really at the end of the road, although it was.
And the road wasn't all that long either. It depends entirely
upon your point of view; upon what the weather's like and
how comfortable your boots are and whether you're riding
a bike or flying an airplane or running away from a mad
dog. On the window it said in fancy script: *Home-baked
pies fresh daily*. So Sam walked in. I mean, coming upon a
sign like that away out here! It was like finding a fresh-
water island in the middle of a salt-water sea.

Inside it had the same kind of feeling as Mr. Hopgood's
barn. Oh, a wonderful place, a wonderful sight to behold;
like an Eastern bazaar where travelers on camels might step
down to spend an hour, or explorers might buy supplies,

or exotic people in exotic clothes might speak exotic lan-
guages around the door, or exotic creatures like Afghan
hounds might lie and growl. Oh, to step inside and come
upon it by surprise. Things must have been there undis-
turbed for years and years and years, as if arranged for a
special occasion and no one had arrived. Nothing was meant
to be disturbed, oh nothing was ever meant to be sold. It
would be awful for those things to be wrapped up and
taken away, no matter how much money people left behind in exchange.

Oh, what a place to find at the end of a long, long road.
And oh, the smell of it: cinnamon and salt and bread and
apples and vinegar and cedar and linseed oil and cloth and
cane and flour and honey and clean black iron and who
knows, maybe even gold.

Someone moved, but no one came.

Life was there, but not to be seen. *Mysterious* life; you
know? Like life underground or inside the kitchen wall or
just over the edge of your midday dream. There were clank-
ings as of weights going onto scales or coming off them,
and rustlings as of brown paper bags being opened for things
to go inside. There were scufflings and scrapings and shuf-
flings and slappings as of butter being patted or sugar in
packets being thumped down to make room for more. Or
were they animals out of Beatrix Potter heard when you
were very small? Animals living half-human lives? Oh, great
imaginings.

Who would come? Hey? If he dared to call?

A Turk with a flat curved knife tucked in his cummerbund?
An Indian in a turban? A Chinese in a dragon gown? A little
old man with rimless glasses like Mr. Vale and white calico
apron and stooped shoulders and droopy mustache stained

yellow-brown from half a million cigarettes in fifty years? Who could say when you couldn't see? A little old lady with a sweet smile or a large middle-aged lady with a jolly bosom bounce, or a sinister kind of man with a big belly and a red neck and no hair? Or a Tibetan? Or a Russian? Or a Kurd? Oh, Sam had always longed to see a Kurd.

He said, "Is anyone there?"

A head appeared around a tea chest—like a Punch and Judy show on its side. Oh my goodness. Oh my goodness. It was a girl.

"Hullo," she said.

"Hullo," said Sam.

They looked at each other for a while, then she *emerged*. And for a while longer they looked each other up and down.

Goodness. I mean to say! *Another* girl making him flutter about inside. And so different from little Rose and grown-up Rose and Sally who never said a word, so different from all three. She was thirteen or fourteen or fifteen—it didn't matter—much the same as Sam. She had large brown eyes and flour on her nose. It was strange. He had not expected to see another girl. Not so soon. Maybe not for a year, or two years, or until he was twenty-four. He was still getting used to the idea that he'd not be going back for Sally until he was Samuel Spencer Collins, the same, first to fly an airplane nonstop across the Poles. If he had not made that resolve he might never have reached the general store. He might have turned round and gone back to Sally hours before. Even the things you wish you hadn't done are important sometimes. Yeh, thought Sam profoundly, everything pushing on you all the time, getting you there, where you're going.

"Can I help you?" said the girl.

Why was it that he had come inside? Gawd, there had been a reason, hadn't there?

"Oh, yes," Sam said, remembering. "I've come in for a pie."

"What sort of pie?" said the girl.

"A meat pie," said Sam, surprised in tone, as if she should have known. (Was there any other kind, except apple and cherry and rabbit and raisin and curry and lemon and custard and bacon and mince with potato on top?)

"You can't get one here," she said.

"It says so on the window outside."

"That was a million years ago," said the girl, "before I was alive. That was in the olden days when everyone was digging for gold. Auntie Flo used to bake them. She doesn't now."

"Why?"

"She died."

"You can get them somewhere else, can't you?"

"Who'd want them if we did? All the goldminers have gone away. Almost everyone's gone away. Who'd we sell them to?"

"Me."

"But who's seen you before? I haven't. Keep pies here just for you and no one knows you and you've never even bothered to call in before to say hullo? What if we'd got them in last year? They'd be stinking by now."

"That's a silly thing to say," said Sam.

"What's silly about it? Have the place stinking up with rotten pies waiting for you to walk in the door? That's not silly: that's hygiene. You wouldn't buy them if we had them. You'd take one sniff and run a mile. You'll have to have something else. What about a chocolate bar?"

"Gawd, you don't live on chocolate bars. Do you? Do you live on chocolate bars? I want proper food. I want something like a pie."

"No pies. I've told you that. People don't ask for pies. If they want a pie they make their own."

"Well, I can't make my own."

"Are you stupid or something?"

"Of course I'm not stupid. But I don't know how to make a pie. Gee whiz, even my mum gets in a knot with the pastry. Anyway, I haven't got a stove."

"Why haven't you got a stove?"

"Because I haven't, that's why. Where would I put it? What would I do with it? A proper freak I'd look, staggering along the road with a stove on my back. And where would I get a chimney from?"

"Buy one from us."

"You can't buy chimneys."

"Oh yes you can. We've got them out in the yard. Two of them. Real beauties. Made out of iron. Dad says they've been there since he was a little boy. They're going real cheap."

"Well, I'm not your bunny," said Sam. "I'm not buying your blooming old chimneys that you've had for a hundred years. How would I carry a chimney as well as a stove? Anyway, you've got to have all sorts of things to make a pie, I know that much, and I've got nothin'. You've got to have a house to start with, to put the stove and the chimney in."

"Haven't you got a house either?"

"Of course I haven't got a house. Strike me, I'm only fourteen. You've got to be married before you have a house."

"Who told you that?"

"Everyone."

"They never told me. I'm not married. I've got a house."

Sam made a soprano kind of squeak. "Well, I haven't. All I've got is tenpence and you can't buy a house for tenpence."

"You can buy some stale biscuits though. Golly, you can buy millions for tenpence if you buy them from me. I'll give you a real big bag. We can have a clearance sale! I'll give you a sack full. And some of them aren't even properly soft yet. Some of them haven't even got weevils in them yet."

"Gawd," said Sam.

"Sell you some apples, then. Real cheap. You can cut out the brown bits."

"I don't want your rotten apples and I don't want your rotten biscuits. I don't want your rotten anything. I told you, I want a nice pie."

"And I told you we haven't got any pies. And they'd have been rottener than the apples and rottener than the biscuits, just waiting for you to call. Why don't you take some potatoes? Best seed potatoes. Going real cheap. Light a fire somewhere and cook them in the coals. They'll be beaut after you knock off the eyes and chuck away the mushy ones. What about some carrots? Scrub the dirt off and eat them raw. What about some fruitcake? Only came in last month. What about some butter and a loaf of bread? What about a tin of beans? They're going extra cheap because the tins keep exploding all the time. Dad says they'll kill someone if we don't get rid of them soon. No one's been buying beans since the goldminers went away."

They looked at each other again for a while.

No one came.

It was nice. Nice being there. Nice talking to her. Nice looking at her. It was, you know. Real nice.

Sam felt warm inside from the warmth that was glowing all around her. A lovely curl fell over one eye, and her voice was extra special, as if you were hearing it inside. Extra special. There must have been a better way of describing it, but not for the moment. She was teasing him, of course, and he didn't mind. But never a smile. Never a smile from her. She played it as straight as a deadpan comedian. She was different from other girls. Or maybe there were all *kinds* of girls. Sam blinked from the shock of the thought. All kinds, just like boys!

"What's your name?" he said.

"Mary." Suddenly she looked shy.

He thought about that, too, and she gave him time to think about it. *Mary* was right for her. Just perfect for her.

"What's yours?" she said.

"Sam."

They were beginning to frown at each other. Strange. Oh, so strange.

"I feel bad about not having a pie for you, Sam."

"That's all right."

"Why haven't you got a house, Sam?"

"I've left home."

"Did you have a row then?"

"No."

"Does anyone know where you are? Does your mum know?"

"I've written her a letter. I've posted it today. Well, Bernie posted it."

"Who's Bernie?"

"A friend of mine, I suppose."

"Aren't you sure if he's a friend?"

Sam slowly shook his head, thinking about that as well. Thinking about everything, really. "He never spoke to me, you know. Never said a word to me. Neither did Sally. I wonder why? I'm not hard to talk to, am I?"

"Where are they now?"

"A long way. A long way."

He pointed absently, back, away, as if not sure about any of it, as if he might have been wondering if it had happened at all, and Mary seemed to be pleased about that.

"Where are you going next, Sam?"

"Gippsland, I reckon."

"What are you doing when you get there?"

"I don't know. Dig for gold, maybe. Sit under a palm tree, maybe. Ride a horse, maybe. Get a job if there are any jobs around. I reckon Gippsland sounds beaut. Things to eat, you know, just sticking up out of the ground. I'm not worrying. I'm not worrying. True, I'm not."

Oh, she was different from Sally and little Rose and grown-up Rose, though he was not sure how.

"Why don't you stay here?" she said.

"You mean *here*?"

"Why not? It's lovely here. Loveliest place in the world. You'll never find anywhere better than here."

"Won't I?"

"You haven't got a hope. My dad's been all over the world. He's been to Egypt and Gallipoli and France and England. Been to the Isle of Man too. He says there's nowhere like here."

"That's different," said Sam.

"What's different about it?"

"Because it's his home. If a fellow makes up his mind to go, he's just got to go."

But that would be leaving Mary, wouldn't it? Perhaps he shouldn't do that. Staying close to her mightn't be a bad idea.

"Are you on your own?" he said.

"Until Dad comes home. Today's his day for orders, for taking them around. But he won't be long. He's never later than five."

"Where's your mum then?"

"She died when Auntie Flo died. Just about everyone died, they say. It was the flu."

"Gee, I'm sorry about that."

"It's all right. I was only two."

"And you've been alone all that time?"

"I've got my dad."

Sam hadn't meant it that way. (Or had he? He wasn't sure.) But it didn't matter. "And you're safe," he said, "when he leaves you? When your dad leaves you all on your own?"

"Well, you'll not be hurting me, will you?"

"Of course I won't be. I'd look after you. I'd fight them off to save you."

"Fight off who?"

"I don't know. But things happen, don't they? Mrs. Hopgood seemed to be worried about Sally. I think she was worried about me."

"Why? What would you be doing to anyone?"

There they were. On the water. Seen. There they were, waiting to die by Sam's hand—Flying Officer Samuel Spencer Collins, the same, captain of Sunderland flying boat B.

There they were, suddenly seen as clouds parted and a world of mist changed to a world of ocean gray and green.

Came the gunner's sharp report into the headphones against Sam's ears: "Nose to Captain. Object on the water. Starboard bow. Fifteen degrees. Six miles." (The voice of Robert Sydney Lyons, Roman Catholic, aged nineteen, of Blackwood, South Australia, twelve thousand miles across the earth removed from where his mother turned in her sleep and opened wide her eyes. Robert Sidney Lyons speaking his last words and his mother very nearly heard.)

"Nose to Captain," Robert said. That was all he had to say. "Object on the water. Starboard bow. Fifteen degrees. Six miles." His *last* words. You'd think they'd have done better for him than that. If you're going to die they ought to let you know, ought to give you a minute or two to prepare, to think up something befitting the occasion. After all, dying's an important thing to do, when you're any age—ninety or nineteen or just a couple of days.

Sam knew what the object was, of course. Oh, he knew all about it, and exactly where he, Sam, fitted in, too. It was the fishing vessel, the tuna fisherman, with booms spread like dragonfly wings, graceful and sweeping on the gray-green sea, exactly where the Operations Officer had said it would be.

Sam had known. He had known all day. He had known even before they got him out of bed. Maybe it was the day for warning the Protestants and catching the Catholics by surprise.

"Thank you, Nose," said Sam. "I see it."

So calmly he said it—that was Sam's way—but inside he was tearing with fright and with pain. It had been coming, you see. As sure as the sunrise. As sure as midday. Inside he already knew the pain, knew the agony, knew the going away. But a fishing vessel; a miserable, lousy fishing vessel; not a magnificent battle gesture in the sky.

The fishing vessel with Germans aboard, fishing not for tuna but for Sunderlands and Wellingtons and Liberators and Whitleys and everything else in which British or Americans flew. That's what it was supposed to be—but could you swear? Who could be utterly sure? The Operations Officer seven hundred miles astern—at his desk surrounded by paper and forms? He didn't have a *doubt*—all he had to do was sling his orders around. It was all free for him. Free of worry. Free of risk. Free of care. He didn't have to press the bomb button. He didn't have to fire the guns. He didn't have to die with his lifeblood on his hands. But for Sam in the sky, poised two thousand feet above the sea? For Sam was the act of the killing—for the Operations Officer was the plan.

"We are certain of it," the Operations Officer said, eight hours ago, pointer in his one hand at the end of his one arm, tapping the huge map on the wall. "Certain. Certain now. The signals are absolutely clear. They are using fishing vessels as fighter control and steps have been taken to warn the neutrals away. We've warned them in every way we can. We've bent over backward; perhaps compromised security; that's the absurdity of this Command. Any honest fisherman fishing there is mad, plain bloody mad, and risks his own neck. His blood is on himself, not on you. Any honest man left out there now is a fool. Every tuna fishing vessel you see is your legitimate target as a fighting man to attack and destroy. Drop your bombs and fire your guns and have faith in the people here. We know. We're sure. Is it to be the enemy or is it to be you? How many more aircraft are we to lose? How many more crews are not to return? No false sense of chivalry, please. I don't understand this philosophy; this gentleman's approach to war. They are not fishermen, not fishermen at all. Do I make myself clear, or do I have to dance up the wall? The more they look like fishermen the less likely it'll be. They're not Frenchmen or Spaniards or Portuguese. They are the Luftwaffe, your enemy in the air. They are enemy fighter control with transmitters directing squadrons of enemy fighter aircraft specifically onto you. To make shark bait out of you. There are crews on this station who fight this war as if the enemy were a visiting cricket team.

Saluting him with your wings. Does he ever do it to you? Dropping him dinghies and food packs after you've shot him down—precious materials supplied for your own survival. Does he do the same for you? Why bother in the first place if you help him live to fight again to kill your brother. This is not a game on the playing fields of Eton or Melbourne Grammar School. My arm is in that sea. You want to join my arm? You want to get down there with it among the sharks? Is that the way you want it? The enemy is out there to kill you. He knows what he's fighting for; his head's screwed on right; he's out there to mangle you. Killing you is what his war is all about. If you sight him, return the compliment, please. Attack and destroy. Or, my beauties, that's what he'll do to you."

Sam sounded the warning horn.

That sound to alert the crew, that blaring sound they could hear above engine noises and every other thundering sound.

"Captain to all positions," said Sam. Oh, so calm was his voice when he switched on the microphone. So calm he was, reminding them systematically of all the things they had to do.

Down he went toward the sea, power increasing, noises building up to a fever of sound, bomb doors opening, bombs trundling out beneath the wings like black barrels. Gunners testing guns with short bursts of fire; checking sights, checking turret hydraulics, settling down. Only a fishing vessel. A piece of cake, this'd be. Wireless operator, finger on the transmission key, sending out the signal to tell them back home, to send the Operations Officer whooping round the room. But something was wrong.

Something was not right inside Sam.

Oh, what was he doing here? He had not flown yet across the Poles, and he was already twenty-four. Well, you break things down as you go; you don't do everything you set out to do; and if you did, would Sally care? Would she even know? Or would Rose? Or Gwendolyn in the canoe? Or Jane on the train? Or Agnes by the sea? Or Hannah by the waterfall?

Oh, what about tomorrow? Something was wrong with tomorrow. Something was wrong with it now because it wasn't there for Sam to see. There are times when you know. Times when the present is not real and years of long ago lie too clearly revealed.

"Control to Captain." That was Johnny, up on top of the Sunderland, speaking from the astrodome, that clear Perspex dome up high from where he presided over action like a god on a throne. "They've opened fire, you know. That's cannon. That's pretty heavy stuff, Sam. They've got cannon mounted in the stern. They must be very jumpy, the silly so-and-sos, or else they know we know. That's bad, Sam."

Well, certainly stupid, thought Sam. As stupid as could be. To have cannon there concealed, but to give the game away too soon. They'd have nailed me better if they'd waited a while. Or are their nerves all shot up like mine? I might have held my fire. I might have, you know. I mightn't have dropped the bombs. I hadn't really made up my mind. I might have flown on down the side and let them go with not a shot fired and nothing compromised. If they'd kept their guns covered, it's not likely we'd have spotted them. Or is it as Johnny says—they know we know? Can they see my eyes?

"Control to Nose," Johnny said, from up there. "Open fire at a thousand yards."

Tracer shells were lying like paint streaks in the sky,

lovely lazy lines of enemy fire curving up and curving by, puffs of blackness in the air like hiccups, streaks of red and yellow and a fierce, tearing pain that Sam had known about, in a way, for years and years. He had felt it first under the tram.

"Control to Captain. Take evasive action, Sam. Don't leave it too late, Sam. Undulate, Sam, for God's sake. Control to Nose, come on there, Robert, open fire will you! Midships, can you bring your guns to bear? Sam! Sam! For God's sake don't charge them like a battering ram. What's going on down there? Can't anyone hear?"

Oh, a blinding, tearing pain inside Sam, the threshold where pain is so great you stop feeling it any more.

"What about some fruitcake then?" Mary said. "It's very good cake. Not stale at all. Dad says it's like wine, gets better if you keep it for a bit. It's got lovely cherries in it. I won't charge."

"That would be nice," said Sam.

"You like fruitcake? You really like it?"

"I'd say so if I didn't. Yeh, I like it."

"And what about Gippsland? Are you going there to-night?"

"Well, I can't, can I? Even if I wanted to. Even if I tried. It's not close enough for getting there tonight, is it?"

Mary seriously shook her head. "It'll rain, too. Rains every night round here in the winter. Down it comes. You'll get awfully wet walking along the road."

"I'm not even thinkin' of it, Mary. I never even meant to. I'd be having a sleep somewhere."

"Where?"

"I don't know where, but I'd be looking soon. Pretty soon now. Old Mo told me not to go too far, not to go too late.

Always to find a place before it was dark. And not to go crawling up hollow logs or anything. Where am I now?"

"Don't you know?"

"Would I be asking if I did?"

"Fancy you saying it wasn't the best place in the world and not even knowing where you were. You've got a cheek, you have."

"Hey?"

"I reckon you've got a hide a foot thick. It's Staines. That's where you are. Named after the family. After my granddad. That's me, too, till I'm married. Mary Staines. Then I wonder what name I'll have?"

She was looking at Sam—straight at him in the eye—and he wasn't ready for thoughts of that kind. Though it'd be interesting, wouldn't it? She'd be fun, which was more than you could say for some of them.

"Didn't you see it outside?" she said. "*Staines Store. Established 1883.*"

"I only saw the bit about pies," Sam said. "I've never heard of Staines before."

"Never heard of it!" Not really a question. Nothing but blank astonishment.

"Has anyone?" Sam said.

"Of course they have. Everyone has. Except you. How'd you get here, then, if you've never heard of us before?"

"I didn't have to know anything about you. I walked along the road and you came."

"Did I?" she said. "I don't remember going anywhere."

"You know what I mean!"

"Where did you walk from?"

Sam sighed. "Miles and miles and miles. From Macclesfield Road. Wherever that is."

"What were you doing at Macclesfield Road?"

"Gee whiz," Sam said. "I reckon you take the prize. You do, you know. You take it. I had to be somewhere, didn't I? I can't appear out of thin air, can I? I stopped the night there. I got a ride in Mr. Hopgood's truck. I just stop here and there. Like a gypsy. I just come and go. I don't care where. I slept under a church once. The whole night, too. I'm a swaggie."

She scoffed. "You're not a swaggie."

"I am. I ought to know."

"You haven't got a swag. You haven't got a blanket or anything. You haven't got whiskers even. You'll die of cold, that's what'll happen to you. You'll get pneumonia or something because you haven't got your mum to tuck you in at night." She was smiling at him. "Swaggies only come here for the summer. They're like the flies. In the winter they go away. You can't get anyone to split a log of wood round here once June comes around. You're not much of a swaggie."

"I'm a very good swaggie, and I'll split wood for you any old time. I'm good at splitting wood. I'm extra good at chopping trees down. You should have seen me in the snow with Mr. Hopgood's ax. I really swung it around. It was terrific chopping trees."

"I'm scared of swaggies; I'm not scared of you. Dad wouldn't leave me here on my own if he knew any swaggies were around. And Dad always knows. There's nothing round here my dad doesn't know. You're not a swaggie; you're only a boy running away. How'd you go in the snow?"

"All right," Sam said testily. "I went very well, I reckon. And I thought you were going to give me some cake before I fall down dead on the floor."

"I'm getting round to it," she said. "But cake's not much good if you're dying of hunger."

"Well, you offered it. I didn't ask for it, did I?"

"Don't you want it?"

"Of course I want it."

"Well, don't sound as though you don't care. You'd be better having a pie, though."

"Oh my gawd," said Sam, "isn't that what I've been saying all along?"

"I could make you one, I suppose."

"It'd take hours!"

"Does it matter how long it takes?"

"Well, I can't hang round all night waiting for it."

"Why can't you? You said you weren't going anywhere. You can sleep in the storeroom if you like. If you promise not to take anything. It'd get me into trouble if you did. You'd be warm in there, too. You'd be dry. You wouldn't catch cold in there, Sam, and the rats are nowhere near as bad as they used to be. Only half the size. No bigger than cats now. Dad put that new poison down. Don't you go licking it up off the floor, though."

"Strike me," said Sam. "Am I likely to be doing that?"

"I don't know. But you're talking about your belly a lot, aren't you? I don't know what you'll be doing. I don't know what your habits are. Do you want to stay or don't you?"

"What's your dad going to say about it?"

"Nothing, if he doesn't know."

"You told me there wasn't anything he didn't know!"

"Well, there won't be anything to know if you don't get caught. So don't go snoring too loud or anything. Don't go making noises that wake up the dogs—or you won't be eating anything. They'll be eating you."

"If I can't go making noises, how am I to get my pie?"

"What pie?"

"The one you're baking for me!"

"Where'd you get that idea? Pies are no good for you. You want something better than a pie. I'll smuggle you up some dinner when I put out the dog scraps."

Sam was feeling a bit confused. "I can see it coming. I can, you know. A mile off. The dogs'll get the dinner and I'll get the scraps."

"Well, are you staying or aren't you?"

"I suppose so," sighed Sam.

"You don't have to do me any favors, you know."

"I'll *stay*," yelled Sam, "and thank you very much."

"That's right," she said, "shout your head off. Tell everybody in the district."

"Tell who? I haven't seen a soul. I haven't even seen a horse or a cow. I mean—a shop away out here. Whoever comes into the place?"

"You did, didn't you?"

"Yeh. But who else?"

"Me dad. And he'll be coming in pretty soon. You'd better get out there. Out the back. You'd better get yourself up the ladder and into the loft and settled before he comes busting in here. You want something to read?"

"What've you got?"

"Got the *Woman's Mirror*. Got some newspapers. Got the *Australian Journal*."

"That'll do," said Sam.

"What'll do? The *Woman's Mirror*! You won't be able to see much. There's no light."

"Oh gawd," said Sam. "You sure change direction. I hope there'll be enough light to eat by."

"You're not going to tell me you don't know where your mouth is! You'd better get up that ladder, I think. If Dad comes home and finds you he'll chop your head off. He doesn't like boys hanging around. Not round me. He knows too much about them, I think."

Sam thought about it for a while; looked her up and down again for a while; thought of the cold outside for a while; then went out into the storeroom at the back and climbed the ladder.

A very interesting situation, Sam thought; yes, by crikey. There'd never been one like Mary Staines. Never be another either.

Twenty-one

LATER, SAM reckoned the hours between five o'clock and eight were only a low-key torment when he lined them up against the drama of what came after. "Strike me," Sam said to himself. "Strike me," he kept on saying, half the night long. "Oh strike me."

There he was, not so long since, zipping down Riversdale Road hill with sixty-four *Herald*s over the bar of his bike, minding his own business, whistling a tune—and *bang*. It was on. Suddenly the world is a dangerous place.

He put himself up there, into that loft, and lay low, glowing for a couple of minutes like something overcharged with electricity. It's a wonder he didn't light up the place and cast shadows! This could have been an epoch-making brink. Oh brother, could it ever. Even after her dad came home just on five (making the timing of that escape up the ladder about as fine as a slither), she still managed to bring him a couple of newspapers and the promised hunk of cake—not that he could see the words, or the cake either, if it came to that. He might as well have been in a cave somewhere. She couldn't have been sparkling with intelligence, now could she? Bringing him papers to read in the dark! The only direct light was a watery chink getting in at what looked like the edge of the door they opened to toss out the hay or straw or whatever it was they had stacked in this loft—or maybe it was the door they had opened fifty years ago to toss the stuff *in*, because everything smelled old (really *old*) and there was an awful great heap of it, as if it hadn't been disturbed since the Land Boom or the Gold Rush. After all, who'd be buying hay these days? All that grass growing everywhere, as free as air. If you were a horse, you had only to put your head down and get stuck into it—and if you were too stupid to help yourself, who'd own you for the pleasure of paying your hay bill, anyway?

It was *good* feeling Mary's weight hit the ladder, coming up his way, and remembering in a second everything she'd said earlier. But what about the rats? It wasn't the easiest thing picking where that girl left off teasing and started talking straight.

"Here," she whispered, "your newspaper and your cake. That's my dad. He's back. So don't go striking matches or climbing down the ladder, no matter what, or sneezing or anything. I'll be back later."

"Hey!"—but she'd gone! So how was he to see? That dumb girl. Wait for summertime?

Rats as big as cats! I mean, they'd eat you alive, lick their chops, and spit out the bones. But there wasn't a rat smell even when you sniffed down near the bottom of your lungs. Old grass was the smell up here (good sneezing material), like those paddocks out past Mont Albert school waiting for autumn rain. Oh, very old grass, and enough of it lying round loose to gather up to make a soft spot in a safe place back from the edge. By then Mary's dad was thumping about below like a regiment getting ready for home leave. He must have been the biggest man on earth. The floorboards *groaned* as he walked over them. No wonder no one came bothering Mary. He'd eat you for breakfast! Catching one thirty-fifth of a glimpse of him over the edge with one thirty-fifth of an eyeball was like sighting a bull elephant running wild when all you've brought is your peashooter and you've eaten the peas. How could such a mountain of man-flesh have such a willowy-looking daughter? The propagation of the human race is a wonderful arrangement. Trying to get used to the idea of your own dad is hard enough. Matching up an elfin girl like Mary with that hulking great brute is impossible, mate.

That handsome kid in the wooden cradle rocking.

Oh, getting used to the idea that you've joined the human race and proved yourself. Just accepting that you've made with her a new human life big enough to hold in your hands, big enough to give the world to, big enough to let you know that your own life goes on in visible form. Marvelous. Marvelous. (That assurance you badly need.) And she had borne the pain to make this life with you. Yes, Sam; he looks the way you did—but has also the look of her.

Going back to that girl, after all those years. Going back looking for her. Out of all the girls ever born, going back for her. And finding her there.

"Never, Sam; you'll never find her," Mum said. "It's a dream."

"She said she wanted to see castles on the Rhine. What if she went? What if she got trapped there by the war?"

"If she did or if she didn't, Sam, it's her life, not yours. You're not being mature about it; you're being a romantic boy. Everyone's gone crazy, everyone's mad with this war. All these strange things you say. You'll never find a girl who was there all those years before. You'll look at her and you'll wonder why, why, what did I see in her? Or she'll be married to someone else. Or she'll not be your kind—hard as nails. She'll be different from the person you knew. Going back, Sam, is not the way; you're too serious with your girls. Do you want to break your heart again—or hers? Going back is looking for dreams and when you open your eyes a dream isn't there."

"She's the one. The only one out of them all."

1940 that was. Oh, what a year. Marrying her.

Doors below were being shut then, and bolted. Those shop-door bolts shot home like greased rifle bolts. As if next moment someone would be aiming a rifle (just cocked) and he'd be dodging the bullets. As if he was *locked* in, mate. Yes, sir. As if he'd made a serious tactical error somewhere. As if this lean girl and her vast father had lured him to destruction. As if step by step this had been preordained and he'd walked into it like hundreds before him and he'd be spending the rest of his life in chains, working down in the salt mines. They'd be lifting a trap door somewhere and chucking him down. And down. And down. And there'd be this great chasm deep in the earth with lights glistening on salt crystals and hundreds of kids swinging picks and chanting rhythms like galley slaves. Well, why not?

I mean, he was a million miles from anywhere and not a living soul but her knew where. What if she forgot? What if she never came back? What if the whole place were a projection of imagination into which unwary mortals, lured by promises of pies fresh daily, slipped without knowing they were falling. Well, all that fog lying about, and the smells of the place, and the look of it, and the age of it. It was like the Arabian Nights, right enough, even to the maiden, though she wasn't wearing houri pants, one had to admit. But everything was locked up, wasn't it! And bolted. And barred. As if they'd gone away not meaning to come back for a couple of years or a couple of centuries. "Don't make a noise," she had said, "or the dogs will eat you." "Don't strike matches." "Don't come down the ladder." "*No matter what.*" Don't breathe, don't sneeze, don't snore. All sorts of prohibitions. What would he invoke? Demons? Rats as big as cats? Earthquake? Doom?

Where was the house? Where had they gone, that mountainous man and the elfin maid? Where was the stove she was cooking the dinner on? Couldn't smell smoke. Couldn't smell dinner. By crikey, if a fire happened, he'd burn to death; if a ghost walked, there'd be nowhere to run; if he wanted to go to the lavatory—well, that was something he'd better not start thinking through.

It was all but *black*, you know, and it wasn't supposed to be night yet. Couldn't have been a minute later than half-past five. And rain started on the roof as Mary had said it would, and those dogs outside got stirred up over something and sounded like caged wolves. Ordinary *fierce* wasn't the word. . . . But he couldn't seriously worry about it, not yet. All he could feel was fascination. Just sitting there, he was, in that *fantastic* shop, on his little heap of straw, gnawing at his hunk of cake with a silly look on his face. Not that anyone was there to observe his face (except djins and genii), but Sam could feel the silly look growing into a wider and wider grin until he couldn't go on eating cake because it started dropping out of his mouth. Oh, boy. And later she was coming back! But after two more hours he was still sitting there and the grin had gone somewhere else and he was feeling round carefully for crumbs in case he had lost any and he was listening hard for rats—or spirits—or whatever else it was that lived in places like this after the lights went out. And *aching*. Every muscle and sinew and bone ached from stiffness and cold and simple basic fright.

Oh, it was as black as black ever knew how to be—and all around him, unseen, were a thousand leftover pieces of generations of years. Oh, in the light of day that shop sparked off exciting imaginings, but in the dripping intensity of night there were creeping sensations and awarenesses that had him sitting up straight and aching sick.

Leaving the Hopgoods had been mad. He could have settled in there for days. Weeks maybe. He could have worked with Bernie down in the mine. He could have been mining for gold, for real gold, like a real man, and eating terrific food and sleeping in a warm bed and having Sally to look at to cheer him up and every now and then going for a drive in the Talbot, to market maybe, with a load of cabbages that would bring a world record price of ten shillings a dozen and everyone would walk tall and proud.

Twenty-two

A METALLIC sound sent a flash of fright through Sam. It couldn't possibly have been a key turning in a lock, but that's all it was. A heavy door opened—no squeaking, no groaning

—opened smoothly on oiled hinges and admitted a ray of light making a human shadow. Oh, a grotesque, moving, looming, swaying, sinister kind of shadow. But it was she. It was nothing coming up from Hades after all. In she came through the opening along the ray of light, bearing with her a tray and an aroma of braised meat that at once turned all Sam's aches and urges into a single gigantic longing to follow his nose and get down to business.

"Are you up there?" she said.

"Yes."

"He's gone."

"Who's gone?"

"Dad. To the Progress Association Meeting. Once a month they meet. I forgot. So I waited till he went. I thought that was best. There's enough light to see by, but come down backward or you'll fall."

"I'm frozen," said Sam.

"What are you frozen for?"

"Because it's so hot up here."

He went down backward as prescribed, stiffly, grumbling —though not seriously meaning the grumbles. It was so marvelous that she had come.

"And all that hay to keep you warm," she said, "and the newspapers to put over you? Haven't you any brains at all?"

"Nope."

He came level with her, close to her, and felt a wave of body heat, as if an aura of radiation surrounded her. It unsettled him immediately and confused his urges again. He walked stiffly a few steps to the open door, more to escape her than for any other reason. Outside was a small cobbled courtyard swept by misty rain and lit by a hard bright pressure lantern swinging from a bracket over a door a few yards across the way. The shop was much more inviting. He went back to her, aware of the draft, of the dampness and chill.

"Is that your house out there?" he said.

"I'd reckon," she said, "wouldn't you?"

"Where are the dogs?"

"Sleeping underneath it out of the rain. They're better watchdogs when it's fine."

He cocked his head at the loft. "I won't be able to sleep up there, you know. I reckon I'd die."

"Well, you won't be sleeping in the house, so you'll have to die."

"Can't you get me a couple of blankets or something?"

"Gee, you're a real tough swaggie, you are."

"It's so close to the roof up there." His voice was thin. "That's bare iron, you know. Have you ever thought about it? You ought to go up there and put your hand on it and see."

"I oughtn't to do any such thing. You're silly enough for both of us, I think."

"Well, it's cold and you've been such a long time coming."

"My goodness, you do make yourself at home quickly, don't you!"

She had placed the tray on the counter and gone to the other side near the tea chest—that same tea chest around which her head had appeared first of all in the afternoon. "Pull up the stool, Sam, and get on with it. It's a nice dinner if you like beef stew. I could have made it into a pie for you, I suppose."

She was hard to see because the light from outside didn't

reach her now. She was seated at about his own height, or so it appeared from her eyes. Strangely, very strangely, they looked like two pale lamps alive in the night, so they must have been picking up light from somewhere. He was strongly aware of her, oh electrically, but the dinner smelled good. Oh, very good.

"That's hot milk," she said, "in the cup."

"Thank you."

"With some malt in it."

He was sitting there, nodding over it, making broad, deep, and general kinds of sniffs.

"Get on with it, Sam. We haven't got all night."

"I am, I am. Sniffing at it's part of it. Gawd."

"You don't have to swear."

"I'm not swearin'."

"You are. You're doing it all the time. Gawd's swearing. It's taking God's name in vain."

"Is it?" said Sam. "You're just like Auntie."

"Auntie who?"

"My Auntie Frederika Victoria Collins."

"You're kidding."

"I wish I were."

In a while she said, "Dad'll be a couple of hours."

"Yeh?"

"So I'll go about half-past nine."

"Go where?"

"Gee whiz. Back to the house. Where else? To lock up the shop door before he gets back. To be good and safe and sure. Were you expelled from school in the first grade or something? In the morning I'll open up, so you'll be all right as long as you don't show yourself before you're sure it's me."

"Oh, I'll do that all right. I'll yell, 'Hey, mister. This is me. Sam. Wow-eee, you've got some daughter. Have you ever. She hid me up here, she did, and gave me half your dinner, too.'"

"I didn't, you know," Mary said. "I gave you the dogs' share."

"Thank you," said Sam.

"We'll make out you're an early customer, if you like. Then you can ask if you could chop some wood. Would you do that?"

"Yeh."

It was a good, stiff stew with character. Oh, very good. Mum's weren't any better. Mum's had less meat in them.

"It would be good if he let you stay. Wouldn't that be good, Sam?"

"Yeh, I reckon."

"You could be shop boy. You could help me."

"Doing what?"

She giggled, which surprised him. "You like my stew?"

"I'll say."

"There isn't any more, so don't ask for it. You've got the lot, and the scrapings off Dad's plate, too."

Sam wouldn't have cared if he had.

"I'd better get the blankets, I think. Then you'll have them. If he comes home early, I mightn't get the chance again."

He was beginning to wonder whether he would need them. He was feeling snug and warm already, and well fed. Like a fat cat. Almost hot in fact. That stew was sensational. There were spices in it; the sort that made the hair prickle on your scalp and brought you out in a sweat a couple of minutes later. The shop had the same smell. Aromatic. It was an experience, and he was so glad the road had brought him to it. You could pick up the smells one by one if you tried, but when you rolled them together there was Mary's stew right in the middle. Maybe she just carved a hunk off the end of the shop and popped it in the pot with a gallon of water.

Back she came with an armful of blankets.

"Have you finished?" she said.

"Yeh. It was good. Real good. You're a good cook."

"I pass," she said, "but I get sick of it myself. Stew, stew, stew. No imagination. Always stupid stew. If you shin up the ladder, I'll chuck up the blankets."

"Now?"

"You're not reckoning on leaving them down here, are you? You'll go falling and breaking your silly neck if you try taking them up later on in the dark. And that would be the end of us."

"Would it?"

"Don't kid yourself Dad wouldn't hear you fall off the ladder! He's got ears like an elephant. They practically flap. And his bedroom's next to *that* wall of the shop. So remember not to go snoring or grinding your teeth together."

"Gawd," said Sam, "maybe it'd be safer if I left now."

"That's up to you, isn't it?"

But he wasn't interested in going away. Oh no. Not with all that night out there. And not with Mary being so close. It was exciting sensing her personality, those things that made her different from everyone else he had ever met. There was an adventure here—like a journey into a new country. So he climbed the ladder and reached down a long arm and lifted the blankets up, three fluffy warm yellow blankets spattered with rain, and found Mary coming up after them. Which was interesting. Yes. Which he had half expected but was not sure about now that it happened.

"I'll help you make your bed," she said, "so you'll be nice

and cozy and out of sight. I'm a Girl Guide. I know all about making a bed. I make it like cigarette papers tucked into each other. Are you a Boy Scout?"

"I'm a paper boy," said Sam. "I've never had time to be a Boy Scout."

She sat on the edge of the platform, dangling her legs over the side. He could see her profile against the outside light—the profile of her figure and the profile of her face. Oh, she was nice. She seemed to have forgotten about making up the bed, but that was all right.

"It's twenty-five past eight," she said.

"Yeh?"

"So we've got an hour and five minutes left. If he doesn't give you a job, I mightn't see you again, might I?"

"No."

"Will that make you sad, Sam?"

"Yeh."

"There aren't many kids round here," she said, "about two to the mile. A real crummy batch of boys they are, too. They give me a pain, every one of them. And the longer I know them the crummier they get."

"I know what you mean," Sam said.

"Do you?"

"Yeh. It's the same in Wickham Street. No one will be having those girls, you know. They're terrible. They'll be starting an old maids' club in our street about ten years from now with Rose being president, I bet."

"Who's Rose?"

"A crummy little kid," said Sam.

"They'll be starting a club for deadbeats round here, too. Pew. I'll not be having any of them within a hundred yards of me, specially not Sid Cullen."

"What's wrong with Sid?"

"He's always trying it. Never leaving me alone. I can't stand him. But you might be all right."

Sam didn't say anything to that. It didn't need an answer. It sounded pretty good to him just the way it was.

"What are you going to be when you grow up, Sam?"

"A pilot."

"On a boat coming up the bay?"

"Gawd, no. In an airplane."

"Up *there*, you mean?"

"Yeh. And I'm going to fly nonstop across the Poles."

"Go on. You're not."

"I am."

Watching her while she talked was really something; the little movements she made, the girlishness of her that stirred him, the excitement of her. He had never watched a girl so intently before. There she was against the light—soft, shadowy, and knowing he was watching her and acting up to it, too, in a way that quickened his pulse until it caught his breath.

"What are you going to do, Mary?"

"Doesn't matter what I want to do, does it? I'll be stuck here. Dad says he's left me the shop. You know; as if he were crowning me Queen of England or something. Maybe I'm supposed to cheer. I wish he'd leave it to someone else."

"Who else?"

"Anyone. I don't care. As long as it's not me. I want to go to Germany."

"What do you want to go *there* for?"

"To see the castles on the Rhine."

"That wouldn't take long."

"Wouldn't take you long to fly across the Poles either."

"That's different."

"What's different about it?"

"It's never been done before by anybody."

"I've never been to the Rhine before either. It's what you've not done yourself that counts."

It was true, and he found himself frowning about it. But fancy wanting to see castles on the Rhine. Who would have imagined? "Gawd," he said, "I don't think I've ever even thought about them."

"More sense to them, I reckon, than thinking about the Poles. It'd be so cold. You'd properly freeze up there. Worrying about the roof here and wanting to go there! You're nuts."

It was not the *way* she looked that turned him on, but whatever it was that made her into who she was and what she was, that put the lilt in her voice and the sparkle in her that the darkness couldn't hide.

"How about taking me," she said, "in your airplane?"

"To the Rhine?"

"To the Poles!"

"What do you want to go there for?"

"What do *you* want to go there for?"

He frowned about that, too, but if a fellow wanted to fly across the Poles he didn't have to have a reason. "Of course you can't come," he said. "I've got to do it alone."

"On your very own?"

"Yeh. Otherwise it's not worth doing."

"Something's wrong with that," she said, "I don't know what, but it's crazy."

"I don't reckon so—"

"But you'll be lonely. You'll be dead lonely."

"You've got to be. That's the point."

"It's a stupid point, if you ask me."

Slowly she was shaking her head and he knew she was troubled. "Wouldn't you rather I went with you? You could talk to me. I could give you a cuddle to keep you warm. Wouldn't you rather do it with me? Wouldn't you rather see it with me? Wouldn't you rather share it?"

She was serious. There was no teasing any more. And he was holding her hand. There they were, hand in hand. He was sitting beside her swinging his legs over the edge, swinging them back and forth as she swung hers, holding her by the hand. Gee.

"Sam."

"Yeh."

"I wish you wanted to share it. I like you."

"I like you, too, Mary."

"There's lots of time left, Sam. You might change your mind before you get your airplane."

"I might."

"I'd love to see the Poles with you, Sam. I would. I think I'd love to do anything with you."

He could understand that. Doing things with her would be pretty good, too, even seeing castles on the Rhine.

Her movements were bearing closer to him now, the swinging of her legs. The points of contact were warm and secure and oh, so right.

"Sam."

"Yeh."

He was looking at her eye to eye, and he knew what she was saying. He had been waiting for years to hear a girl say it. She was very beautiful—not like a picture or anything, not like a film star, not like anything he had ever really thought about, but beautiful. So he kissed her.

He felt his lips touch. Oh, for crying out loud. Felt her softness, her gentleness, for a second, or for two seconds. Oh, a kiss so light, so soft, so brief, so utterly beyond understanding. They paused, as if waiting for life to get going again, for their hearts to start beating again and their lungs to start breathing again, for their minds to unhook from the stars and return to earth again. So close to each other, so very close, gently and almost silently striking each other with nervous breath. Oh, for a minute or two minutes or five minutes. It was hard to know. Then their noses touched and their chins touched and their cheeks touched, lightly, feather lightly, and they had to draw apart again, hurting too much inside from the stress.

Their eyes came back into view, both his and hers, deep dark eyes, and Sam saw her beauty again, her girlhood, and her hair falling full and fresh; and she saw Sam, a beautiful boy, such a shape to his head, and a soft manliness in the carriage of his head, and strength in his chin and intelligence in his brow.

Sam touched her hair, still flecked with rain, and spilled it from his fingers.

"Mary?"

"Yes, Sam."

So he kissed her again, little by little feeling her press still more firmly against him, little by little feeling the movement of her arms around him and the overwhelming exploding pressure of his nerves and pulse, which made his bruises hurt, though not much. But they broke again, suddenly, and settled heads against each other, arms against each other, hands joined, legs swinging.

"That was my first kiss," Sam said, as if remembering with awe the day he was born.

"And mine."

"Truly? Truly? Was it truly?"

"The first one. Oh yes, Sam. I never did go for kissing those kids."

"Did you like it with me, Mary?"

"Mmm."

"Would you like it again?"

"Mmm."

He kissed her in the hair and on the brow and over the eyes and on the nose and with total deliberation on her lips. It was —oh wow, oh brother—it was out of the world. It was way over the edge. What an edge to go over!

"I think you've kissed girls before. You do it too well, Sam."

"Never," he said. "Oh, never, I swear. A fellow just knows. The same as you know how to kiss him back. But I've imagined it lots and lots of times."

"Are you disappointed?"

"Oh, no, Mary. It's much, much better than imagining it."

"You won't go away, will you, Sam?"

"Why would I want to go away now?"

"You might have to. But you'll always come back to me, won't you, Sam?"

"I'll not be going, Mary."

"There's no one round here. No one like you, Sam. And I know I'll have to stay. I just know. I'm the last of the tribe. It's awful being the last of the tribe. I'll just never get out of this place unless someone like you comes in his airplane and carries me off."

"I haven't got an airplane, Mary."

"You'll be getting it."

"Will I? What hope have I got of getting an airplane? We can't even buy a bike in our house. And all those papers all over the road. The ruin of my life, those papers."

"You'll get your airplane, Sam. I just know."

"You reckon?"

"Of course you will. Of course you will. You've got to

keep on saying it to yourself: I know I will; I know I will. You can do it because I can see it in your jaw. I'll give you the money for the papers, though. You can pay me back any old time."

"I can't take money from you, Mary."

"I don't see why not. From me, more than anyone else, I'd say." She was holding to him tightly. "You'll pay it back; you know you will; and I know you will; any old time, Sam."

He was becoming anxious and uneasy. "How do you know about my papers on the road?"

"You just told me."

"No I didn't. Not the way you said it."

She made as if to separate from him, but he held on hard as if he feared she might jump down and run away.

"How do you know, Mary? I don't mind—truly I don't—how do you know?"

Her voice was small. "It's in the *Argus* and *The Age*. In the papers I passed up to you. Everyone's looking for you, Sam. They're searching the river Yarra and the creeks. All sorts of places. Searching miles and miles away they are. Nowhere near here. How'd you get here, Sam?"

"Oh, gawd. . . ."

"Your picture from your school photograph is on the front page."

"Oh, gawd. . . ."

"Don't you like being famous?"

"Not that way. Oh, gawd. Does that mean they're *dragging* the Yarra? That's miles from where I started out. Do they think I'm dead or something?"

"They wouldn't be dragging it if they thought you were alive."

"What about my mum?"

"Doesn't say anything about your mum. About your dad, though."

"What? What does it say?"

"He says they shouldn't have left you at the side of the road. He says, what's wrong with people? He says people don't care because you're only a paper boy. That if you'd been dressed up in fine clothes they'd have hired a cab and sent you home. He says you've wandered off dazed and come to grief somewhere. He says if you're dead, it's their fault. He says even your money's been stolen and your bike's been smashed to bits and no one picked up your papers. No one cares, he says. . . . I care. I care, Sam."

Sam sat there, hanging onto Mary's hand.

"People have cared, though. Dad shouldn't have said that, Mary."

"I'll always care, Sam; till I die."

Twenty-three

OH, THAT blinding, tearing pain inside Sam that becomes the threshold where pain is so great you stop feeling it any more. And the voices from a long way off shouting inside his head. And the violent helpless hands upon him trying to tear his unmoving body apart in the pilot's seat.

"Get him out of there. Get him out of there. We'll never pull out of the dive."

"Oh, leave me be," Sam cried. "Let me die where I lie."

But they couldn't hear because no sound came out, and the sea was there, seconds away.

"Oh, Mary," Sam cried, "I have to leave you behind."
"Oh, Mary," Sam cried, "till I die."

Twenty-four

A SHADOW bulked in the open door blocking the light from outside. Mary's frightened whisper formed a single word. "Dad."

A single word that became a flame inside Sam. "You said another hour."

"It's Dad."

"What's this door doing open? Mary, are you in there?"

The voice was a bellow. Oh, the volume. It was a wonder the dust in fright didn't flake from the walls.

"Oh my gawd," hissed Sam, and Mary made a kind of reflex jump for the ladder, but missed by a foot, and floundered in the dark with flailing legs, clutching for Sam, clawing for the edge of the platform that went tearing through her fingers, and crashing to the floor of the shop with a wild cry.

Oh, it was so quick. In a second everything changed. In a second it was a different world. There Mary lay, moaning, as if she had lain there for hours.

In came the man. In came the bull elephant. "Where are you? What the hell!"

Mary lay moaning.

"Did you fall from the loft? What were you doing up there?"

"My leg, my leg."

Sam lay flat, flat to the floor of the loft, flat, flat, afraid to breathe, almost afraid to go on living, wishing to turn into a lizard or a piece of straw. Were the blankets hanging over the edge? Were his feet visible from below? Oh, my goodness, she'd said another hour. What was happening down there? None of it could Sam see. Flat on his face, flat to the floor, eyes shut like an ostrich—Mary sobbing about her leg.

"I knew you were up to mischief. Like a cat on hot bricks you were. If that Cullen kid's here I'll chop his head off."

"There's no one, Dad. You know there's never anyone." She was crying—from fright and fear and pain. "Oh, my leg. I've broken it in pieces, I know."

"You've disobeyed—"

"There's no one. No one. It's that terrible possum."

"You mustn't come out of doors."

"It's the possum, the possum. You don't have the mess to clean up. You never understand. Oh, you frightened the life out of me. You made me fall. What did you yell at me like that for?"

"You fell from your own stupidity, you stupid girl. You shouldn't have been there. You shouldn't have left the house. What have we got dogs for? What'll I do with you in bed for a month or more?'

"Set that trap for the possum, that's what you'll do. You'll set it soon enough now that you've got to clean up the mess yourself. I keep on asking and asking. You never take any notice of me. And now I break my leg."

"Your leg's as good as new. Not a thing wrong with it, girl."

She sobbed even louder down there.

"Can't you tell the difference between a break in your leg and a twisted ankle?"

"DON'T SQUEEZE it like that!"

"What a fuss over nothing." Sam heard him sigh. Such a sigh from the soul. "What a fuss, sweetheart." The gentleness in his voice, the softness, the tone. You'd never have imagined it from the man.

"Hang on to me," he said, "you silly little idiot. Mary, the fright you've given me."

He must have picked her up bodily and Sam raised his head to watch him go.

Oh, Mary. Away you go.

From the door did she raise her hand? Did she wave good-by?

He pushed the blankets out of sight under the straw and scuttled for the ladder. Oh, the night out there. Where to now?

The things he had eaten from! They couldn't be left behind exposed. They would betray her—and him—if they were found.

Sam ran for his life, or that was how it seemed to Sam.

Down the road, a minute or two minutes or five, he tossed the plate and cup and spoon into the scrub and hurried on his way as fast as he dared. There was fine rain in his face and the world was so black, so wet, so huge. Where to? Oh, where to now? Heaven knew. Along the center of the road, along the crown, wavering along by instinct, by instinct steering his way, seeing not a living soul.

It was the longest night in the history of the world. All night long Sam walked on and on and on, because there was nowhere to stop, because he had to keep warm, because if he landed here he would never survive. All night long, pushing one leg past the other, all night long flying nonstop across the Poles.

In the morning light he rested against the fallen bough of a tree at the edge of a narrow road that curved through gullies and hills and forest. Ferns grew as tall as palms and ten thousand birds sang simultaneously and water dripped and trickled and bubbled in the earth and the smell was a million years old.

"I'm going to Gippsland," Sam said out loud, "I'm going. I'm going. Mum'll get my letter. She'll get it in a few hours. Then she'll know. When it's time to go, a fellow's got to go."

An ax rang like a bell somewhere. Where was it? Down there?

Sam heard a man singing.